BUILD
UNIVERSES

T.G. SHA

CLOBET VALLEY

The Durbey Dancer

europe books

© 2020 **Europe Books**
europe-books.co.uk

ISBN 978-88-5508-845-9
First edition: March 2020

CLOBET VALLEY
The Durbey Dancer

Title of Game: **Clobet Valley - War of Science**
Free to play- available on Google Play and Apple Store.

To my parents
Vee and Jay

CHAPTER 1

FLOZA THE MISCHIEVOUS

It did not seem like an ordinary day at Clobet Valley: the smell of smoke lingered in the air, covering the sky like dark clouds. The clouds became heavy suddenly; a burst of rain was expected in the valley; it could arrive at any moment and shower the green serene lands.

Floza wondered how it was that the chimneys smoked so often. After all it was summer and hardly any of the fire-places would have been lit by the families of Clobet Valley. She peeked out of her little window, watching the rain drops fall onto the lush lands. In her imagination, she thought it looked a lot like tears falling down from the sky. Floza had a very big imagination; the simplest of things would ignite an idea in her mind. An idea to Floza could become more like an extraordinary dream. She was only fifteen years old, but she was very mature in her thinking. However, at times she would exaggerate certain events – that would cause her to land herself in trouble.

One incident that had got her into 'trouble' was when she told the students at school, she had seen a big black panther at midnight. She had exaggerated to the children at school how the panther was going to attack the entire village.

The children of Clobet Valley attended the Lilly Ann School, which was located high up in the grassy mountains on the edge of the Valley. Lilly Ann had been around since the elders of Clobet discovered the Valley in the 1900's. The children of Clobet Valley loved attending school, as most of their subjects were related to arts and agriculture. The curriculum at Lilly Ann was designed to teach students about survival in the valley, including subjects such as Biology and Zoology.

Floza was quite popular at school but this was due to her mischievous behavior. She was a pale-looking girl, tall in stature for her age, and she wore flimsy dresses. The Headmaster Mr. Nimble always kept an eye on her. Mr. Nimble shared a close friendship with Loops, who was Floza's father. The friends had known each other since the valley was built, so they had shared many years together at Clobet Valley. There were times when Floza was entirely out of control, however Mr. Nimble still took a liking to her; this was the reason she got away with things so often. Headmaster Nimble had known Floza since she was a baby and at times, he would favor her over others, although he would not admit this.

There was however one specific time she had made him so angry that he had refrained from speaking to her for an entire month. The one incident that had driven Mr. Nimble to silence had taken place during the morning assembly. One morning, while all the children were in the school hall waiting for the Headmaster, Floza had suddenly jumped out of her seat and then she started speaking at the top of her voice.

"Attention students! I have something very important to tell you! This is a matter of life and death! We are all going to be eaten by a black panther! I am certain of this because I saw it last night when I peeked out of my window; it looked terrifying! We are not safe at Clobet Valley! I am sure that the panther is going to kill us all!" she announced.

All of the students were stunned; some were panicking, others started crying. It was at that very moment that the students decided they must evacuate the hall, except the Headmaster happened to walk in. Mr. Nimble with a very long beard and the spectacles on his nose were a bit big, in fact much too big for his face!

"What is going on here students?" asked Mr. Nimble.

A freckled-faced boy woke up from his seat.

"Misssss.... Floza has warned us that she saw a big pa pa... panther," stuttered the boy. "She also said that it is going to eat us all!!"

"What? Nonsense!! This is outrageous!" replied the Headmaster. "Now... now.... children, Clobet Valley is well-protected. We have guards on the boarders and we all know that the sighting of a panther would have been reported. Miss Floza has a big imagination!"

The Headmaster then looked at Floza in a peculiar manner and ordered that she leave the school assembly at once. The children were so disturbed after that incident that they missed an entire day of school. Mr. Nimble was furious as this commotion resulted in him losing a day's work.

"Now.... the children were going to be behind in their curriculum."

"How awful!!" thought Mr. Nimble. "That girl's imagination, it's just trouble! I don't know what to do with her anymore. I think... I shall call her father, Loops; he would know exactly what to do."

Although Mr. Nimble had favored Floza at times, he could not excuse today's incident, especially as it had had a negative impact on the students' work. He did feel remorse for Loops however, because he was a single parent, and had to deal with her mischievous behavior. Floza was different; she often dreamt of a world far away from the grassy mountains, a place where people wore hats and spoke in high tones. Life was ordinary for her at Clobet and she wanted more, yet the valley was so peaceful. The people of Clobet Valley were simple folk, always caring for one another. It was an ideal place to live in, a utopian society, a valley where people lived in harmony.

There were no wars, robberies or social disturbances. Instead the people of Clobet were taught to care for one another. On one specific occasion when a boy named Little Jim had got lost in the marketplace, the entire village had found out about it and they had sent out search parties for the boy.

"Thank goodness they found the boy," Floza had thought. "He could have been eaten by that big panther, then at least everyone would have believed me."

Floza worried that it had all been her fault. She was pale and wore flimsy dresses with a ribbon to tie up her wavy hair. She wore a ribbon of different color for each day. Mondays were black; for some reason she felt quite uneasy on this day, maybe because it was ballet practice and this certainly was not her favorite sport. Her father always said, "If you dance like a swan, you will certainly be a graceful lady one day."

But Floza knew nothing about being a lady. She wanted more, she believed the world was bigger than the Annual

Clobet Fair, chasing frogs, or ballet. To Floza her world was much bigger than Clobet Valley.

"Floza come here this instant!" yelled Loops. "I cannot believe this after speaking to you about this over and over again! You just never listen to me!" "Why must I always repeat myself? It was only yesterday that you unlocked the gate at Dr. Hoppin's home, to free his animals. They were his pets! Really now Floza, are you always going to bring trouble to this home? If your mother were here, she would know what to do, but then, she was just like you! Always causing trouble with that imagination of hers."

Floza's mother had died when she was just a baby, she had no memories of her. This was extremely difficult for Loops, who played the role of two parents. Loops tried his best to raise Floza on his own. Still, he felt there was something lacking in his daughter's life – a void he could never fill.

"But father," replied Floza. "I did not make this up, I promise! I really did see a black panther! It was fierce looking, with a very long tail."

"Father, you never ever believe what I say. How can I convince you otherwise? As for Dr. Hoppin's animals, they were going to be slaughtered and you call them pets? How would you feel if Rods was slaughtered?"

"Please young lady, those animals you freed were not your property, and it was surely not your decision to make! We will have this conversation later, and I want you to promise me that you will admit your mistakes. Now get ready for dinner; we are expecting Mrs. Poppsy and her cat. Please, do see that you keep the dog locked away. You do know how Mrs. Poppsy loves her cat."

"Yes, father." replied Floza.

Mrs. Poppsy was the old lady who lived on Cherry Street; she was one of the elders of Clobet Valley. She was quite peculiar at times, and not very welcoming to visitors; she felt they would untidy her beautiful home décor. She lived in an interesting home, filled with china and knitted accessories.

It often felt warm and the smell of baked pies would linger throughout the neighborhood. Mrs. Poppsy always wore floral dresses or attire that was bright and flowery. She had the most beautiful garden in Clobet Valley, it was quite a sight in spring time. Mrs. Poppsy was on time, as usual. Loops had made his special soup with croutons for dinner.

"Floza! Do get the doorbell." said Loops.

Floza ran to the door as if at any second Mrs. Poppsy might leave. She reached for the latch to open the door. On the door step stood an old lady, rather chubby, with a pink flowery dress.

"Good Evening Floza," said Mrs. Poppsy. "Why...little girl, I have not seen you in almost a month. I really do have to apologize, I have been so busy with my garden. You know, sugar plums only grow at this time of year."

"Good Evening Mrs. Poppsy do come in." said Floza.

Floza waited for the old lady to come inside, then closed the door behind her.

"I am sure your garden is looking marvelous. My friend Suzy and I actually get a glimpse of it while walking to school, although I would love to see it close up. Perhaps.... father and I could visit sometime?"

Mrs. Poppsy interrupted Floza as to impose her invitation.

"Why sure little girl. However, you should know that I am incredibly busy planning for the Annual Clobet Fair. I have brought a plum pie for dessert, and do greet Popsicle; you know how he gets around strangers."

Mrs. Poppsy was always accompanied by her cat, Popsicle. Popsicle was a little Persian cat, with a cheeky sort of facial expression that never left. Mrs. Poppsy's husband had died, many years ago and so Popsicle was all Mrs. Poppsy had, since she could not have children. No wonder she treated her pet as if it were a little child. She would knit little scarves for her dear Popsicle. The most 'entertaining' part of this was that it always matched her dress. So, you should not have to guess their attire for this evening's dinner.

"Please tell me you locked that vicious dog up?" said Mrs. Poppsy. "We wouldn't want anyone hurting my little Popsicle."

"Yes Mam, but Rods is actually still a puppy, he is rather small," replied Floza.

"Oh darling! We both know that dogs dislike cats. I have seen the way he looks at Popsicle." said Mrs. Poppsy.

It was a tense moment, of course this always happened when Popsicle was involved.

"I really don't know what the fuss is about," thought Floza. "After all, Rods would not hurt a fly. For some reason, I feel like this is going to be a very long dinner." Rods was a cute little Collie dog, and he loved Floza very much. He was always cheerful, but for some reason Mrs. Poppsy had not taken a liking to him. She felt that he would hurt her little Popsicle. Loops stepped out of the kitchen, with the bowl of pea soup in his hands. He was quite the cook and very welcoming to visitors.

"Good Evening Mrs. Poppsy," said Loops.

"I always tell Floza, the one most important trait is to always be on time."

"Dear Loops, I am sure that taking care of a little girl is not easy; she will need a mother figure at some stage in her life." said Mrs. Poppsy.

"Yes but..." replied Loops.

"No buts Loops," retorted Mrs. Poppsy. "You have to think of the child."

"Well, I guess that I am the invisible person this evening," thought Floza. "The last thing I would ever need is another woman 'replacing' my mother."

15

"I have made your favorite pea soup with croutons." said Loops, so as to change the topic.

"Let's sit down, shall we?"

"I am actually starving, and so is Popsicle!" said Mrs. Poppsy.

She took out a little saucer from her bag and placed it on the floor next to her. "This is for you my dearest." She smiled at Popsicle.

"Incredible how cats get the royal treatment!" thought Floza. "And my poor Rods is outside all alone."

The night turned out well, they told stories of the past and how they planned new developments for the valley. Mrs. Poppsy had left as it was past Popsicle's bed time. She often read stories to him before he dozed off at night. It turned out to be an interesting conversation with Mrs. Poppsy; she was always trying to convince Loops to settle down.

"I really don't see the need for me to get married again," thought Loops. "I think… Floza and I are doing just fine."

Losing Floza's mother had been a painful experience for him; one he wished had not happened. Anyway, Mrs. Poppsy and Popsicle had left, and it was time for bed.

"Floza, you go to bed now," said Loops. "I will do the dishes."

"Yes Father," sighed Floza.

Loops tried his best to play two roles, but he felt he was failing at times. He always looked to his music for inspiration; he played the guitar often and sang songs of tales and great adventures. When Loops was a young man, he had been very curious, and challenged the status quo. He often looked to politics to address his problems, which caused him to land in much more trouble.

His argumentative character had been what attracted Floza's mother to him; she was much like Floza with a big imagination, so both Loops and her mother had complimented each other in many ways.

The night was dark. The wind howled, as if there was a cry for help. Shadows of the trees were seen on the walls of Floza's bedroom. Floza lay in bed; she dozed off, reaching that very moment you cannot explain, when your mind 'sinks' into silence.

She suddenly woke up, to the sound of an animal crying; it sounded much like a cat.

"Meow, meow."

"I must be imagining it," thought Floza. But then she heard it again. The cry seemed to be coming from outside. She pulled aside her blanket, woke from her bed and walked towards the window. She slowly pulled the curtain aside and peeked outside her window. All she could see was utter darkness.

"I think my mind is playing tricks on me," she thought. Just as she was about to question herself, she then heard the cry again. It sounded like an animal crying for help. She stared out of her window, trying to find the "distressed" animal, when suddenly something caught her eye. She saw in the darkness the image of piercing blue eyes. She looked more closely to see what it could be. She had recognized those pair of eyes from before. It was none other than Mrs. Poppsy's cat, little Popsicle!

"What on earth is Popsicle doing outside in the middle of the night?" thought Floza. "Could it be that Popsicle had run away from home? But for what reason?"

She felt terrible to leave the poor cat outside, after all, the cat was all Mrs. Poppsy had.

"I cannot understand what Popsicle is doing outside at this hour?" she mused. "I shall go outside to save it before he wanders off."

Floza opened her bedroom door quietly, so as to not wake Loops. She tiptoed to the door, unlocked it and stepped outside into total darkness. Rods was asleep; if he had seen

Popsicle then the entire neighborhood would have been disturbed. Floza did not want that and no matter how ill she felt of Popsicle, she would hate for him to get hurt in anyway.

She started calling out to Popsicle. "Here kitty, little kitty! Come on, where are you? Remember me....? I'm Floza, Mrs. Poppsy's friend, you were here for dinner earlier," whispered Floza.

There was a moment of utter silence, then she heard an echo through the darkness.

"Floza... Floza...."

"Yes! I know you," said a voice from the darkness.

"I prefer you not to call me kitty," said the voice from the darkness.

"Oh, my goodness, did Popsicle just speak?" thought Floza. "I must be dreaming!" so she pinched herself as to wake up from the dream. "Ouch! that hurts!" She certainly was not dreaming.

"Okay...." replied Floza. "Do come closer, you can stay here for the night, and I will take you to Mrs. Poppsy in the morning."

Floza looked around, waiting for a reaction from Popsicle. There was nothing for a while until to her amazement a black panther stepped out from the darkness. It had a beautiful long tail which waved about, its long whiskers, silvery grey, glittered in the moonlight. But its piercing blue eyes were just like Popsicle's. Floza was stunned, she was standing outside in the darkness at midnight, with a ferocious black panther.

"I can't believe this is happening," stammered the little girl. "I thought you were Mrs.... Popppsy's ca ca catttt. Why did you mislead me?"

"I swear I just saw Popsicle; who are you?" She was so very frightened at the site of the big panther."

"I won't hurt you. I am Edor, Mrs. Poppsy's cat, yes you are correct Floza," said the panther.

"But I have never seen you before!" replied Floza quivering at the site of the big animal. "Mrs. Poppsy has a little Persian ca ca...cattt, you're not little. Why are you avoiding my question? Who are you?"

"As I said little girl, I am Edor, Mrs. Poppsy's cat," said the panther.

"Why have you come here?" asked Floza, trying not to sound frightened by the appearance of the cat. "Was this your plan all along...to EAT me?"

"No, don't be silly little girl. You are not quite my taste, and besides – I have come to speak to you," replied the panther.

"Why do you want to speak to me? I'm sorry. It is rather late, and I must go inside," said the petrified little girl. "I am sure you won't have any difficulty finding your way back home."

"You want answers, don't you?" replied Edor, waving his beautiful tail up and about.

"What do you mean? You don't know anything about me," said Floza.

"But I do! I've known you since you were a little girl. You love Mrs. Poppsy's lemon meringue tart, don't you?" answered the panther.

"Any person can love lemon meringue," replied Floza. "What about your father? Yes. I know him very well," continued the panther.

"What about my father?" she asked.

"Your father Loops! I have known him for a long time. We lived in the same city, had such good laughs. I have wondered as to why he would escape to live in this slow town."

The panther had a sly nature, and he said this with a low snarl in his voice.

"Escape?" asked Floza.

"I meant leave," little girl, he said.

"My name is Floza," retorted Floza, "and for your information, Clobet is a beautiful place. My father has never lived anywhere else, and he met my mother here at Clobet. I don't know why you are lying, but I have to go inside right now!"

"Yes yes, I must leave now," said the panther. "Oh…. and Miss Floza, if ever you were interested in visiting this City, I would be delighted to accompany you."

"No thank you," replied Floza.

"Perhaps it was the same panther that I saw weeks ago?" she thought. "None of the children believed me. I almost got grounded for a month, after all that trouble. When, when… all this time I was right," thought Floza.

Floza wanted so much to see outside of the valley, but she did not trust the cat, not one bit. She ran to her home as fast as she could and quickly closed the door, to make sure she was safe.

"That was a really big cat!!" thought Floza. "It wasn't just any cat… it's a black panther – it looks frightening but what is it doing here at Clobet Valley? And why did it come to visit me? Maybe…. it noticed me, looking at it from the window the night I first saw it? It was talking to me. I can't believe this! A talking panther, and his name is Edor. Edor… that's a nice name for an animal, but how does Edor know my father? He mentioned they lived together in another City, but it can't be. Father would not hide things from me. I know he does not speak much about his past, but I am certain that the only place he has lived in is Clobet."

Floza often wondered why her father never spoke of how her late mother and he had met. Loops was a man of few words, but was fired up with argumentative topics, such as history and politics, not there were any at Clobet Valley; all its inhabitants were like-minded, speaking only of pleasant topics.

The people of Clobet Valley enjoyed the arts; as for Floza, she enjoyed making windmills. She would walk all the way up into the valley, and stick them in the hills. It was quite a sight on a windy day, it illuminated the valley with an abundance of color. The only darkness in the valley was when the sun set, and the people of Clobet dreamt. Their dreams were not of a better tomorrow but that every day would be as peaceful as the present one.

CHAPTER 2

THE CURE

The very next day, all Floza could think about was Edor. She wanted so much to tell her father about her encounter with the black panther, but she felt he would not believe her. The situation was very different for Mrs. Poppsy; she was the one living with a big panther. She was in danger.

"But I don't know how to confront her about this, she loves the cat so much," thought Floza. "I would hate to break her heart, but still I have to tell her. If anything happened to Mrs. Poppsy, I would be to blame, so I have to tell everyone about this. I am feeling so much on edge knowing that we are not safe at Clobet Valley."

It was eight o clock and the little girl from down the road rang the doorbell.

Ring, Ring. She was there to pick Floza up, they walked to school together. Suzy was a few grades below Floza, but she was very mature for her age. She wore big spectacles and her hair was very prim, and there was never a crease on her clothes.

"Wait a moment!" said Loops as he huddled to the door, He hadn't been feeling too well. His back ached and his knees were giving up on him.

"Good Morning Mr. Loops," said Suzy in her squeaky little voice. "Please tell Floza to hurry? I can't afford to miss the morning assembly again."

"What is wrong Mr. Loops? Are you not well?" asked Suzy.

"I am feeling perfectly fine," replied Loops, trying to hide the pain he was feeling.

"Don't worry Suzy. I am on time today," said Floza as she dashed to the door.

"Well girls! Have a good day at school and be sure to pay attention in class," said Loops.

"We will," replied the girls, as they waved goodbye.

Walking to school was quite an adventure; the girls would pass the town where the people of Clobet would sell or trade their goods. Anything and everything could be found at Clobet town and if they were lucky the traders would give them treats as they passed by.

The school bell rang, and all the students hurried to their classrooms.

"This morning's lesson is on endangered species. Children turn to page one twenty," said Mrs. Cordia. It was Zoology class, Floza's favorite subject. She enjoyed learning about different animals, plants and species. "Students… today we are learning about the dodo bird and how it led to extinction. Can anyone tell me where dodos originated?" asked Mrs. Cordia. "Anyone? Well, if you look at paragraph two it clearly states the answer. Now why do I always have to spoon-feed you children?" "Sorry to interrupt, teacher," said Floza. "Can you perhaps tell the class where panthers live?"

"Oh! Come on Flo," said Squiggly, one of the boys in Floza's class.

The children usually called her Flo for short and so did some of the teachers. Squiggly was a thin boy who always sat at the back of the class and never paid attention to his lessons.

He always wore shorts even in the winter months.

"I cannot believe after the last incident you dare to mention the panther again," he continued. "Why, if the Headmaster finds out about this, you will surely be expelled this time," said the boy in a cheeky tone.

"Now, now boy," said Mrs. Cordia. "Don't be so hard on Flo. After all, this is Zoology class and all questions are welcome."

"Yes mam." said Squiggly in a sort of disappointed tone.

"Flo, to answer your question, panthers are members of the cat family, they are found in parts of Persia."

"So mam, what are the chances of having a black panther in our valley?" asked Floza.

"Absolutely zero Flo," replied Mrs. Cordia. "Why…. all we have are squirrels and little kitties," laughed Mrs. Cordia. "No nothing to worry about. Now back to our discussion on the dodo bird."

Mrs. Cordia was very clued up on the subjects she taught. She was a timid and kind lady who often let the students get away with their mischievous behavior.

"Why! If panthers don't exist in Clobet, what is a panther doing here? I can't imagine what would happen if the people of Clobet found out," thought Floza. "What business does a talking panther have here with the people of Clobet? And how does he know of my father? Something very mysterious is going on and I have to find out what it is before someone gets hurt."

Father! I am home, father! yelled Floza, wondering why he was taking so long.

"Just a minute Floza. I am still walking down the stairs," said her father. Floza thought how strange it was that her father was taking so long to get to the door. The door opened and standing there was Loops, paled face and gasping for air.

"Oh, my goodness father! What is wrong? Must I call the doctor? Please tell me!" panicked Floza.

"No child. I will be just fine. No need for the doctor," replied Loops. Just as he was speaking, he lost balance. "No. I don't agree father," said Floza as she called for the doctor. Doctor Hoppins was the town doctor, one of few at Clobet Valley. He was indeed the oldest doctor at Clobet and he was really good at making people better.

"I wish someone could take over my job. I'm getting too old for this," said Dr. Hoppins as he walked into the room.

"Where is your father, child?" asked Dr. Hoppins.

"He is in his bedroom, let me show you," replied Floza. "Dear Loops, now what is wrong my friend?" enquired Dr. Hoppins.

"I just feel a little light headed that's all," said Loops.

The doctor examined Loops.

"Your fever is very high, in fact extremely," said Dr. Hoppins. "If it does not go down in the next ten minutes this is a problem. Your eyes are pale, and you have spots on your body, did you know this?"

"Well I noticed the spots, but I thought it was just pimples," replied Loops.

"How long have you had them for?" asked Dr. Hoppins. "About a month," replied Loops.

"I am going to run some tests for now; I will let you know the result by tomorrow," said Dr. Hoppins. "Floza, for now see that you place a cool towel on his forehead, also this medicine should bring the fever down. Call me if you need anything."

"I will do Sir," replied Floza.

Doctor Hoppins was the famous town doctor and one of few at Clobet Valley. He was very experienced in medicine and produced his own natural-based medicines. Since there were no pharmaceutical companies in the valley, doctor Hoppins treated the patients of Clobet with his originally produced medicines, which worked quite well. Floza had spent the entire night, beside her father.

He did not seem to be getting any better. She was so exhausted that she missed school the next day. Doctor Hoppins visited the next day, and he had brought the test results with him.

"Hi Loops, I can see that you are not looking any better. I am worried Loops, very worried indeed. What I found is that you have a virus. I can't quite pin down what type of virus this is; it seems to be attacking your lungs and your heart is working too fast. You have spots on your body because your blood is reacting to the virus. This is bad Loops. I have these pills to slow down your heart rate. But this is not a permanent solution," said Dr. Hoppins. "I will try my best, but for now you have to stay in bed until your health is restored."

"But doctor, I can't afford to stay in bed, I have to take care of my daughter," said Loops in agonizing pain. "I have to see to her. Who will cook and take care of her?"

"Unfortunately, it is your daughter that will be taking care of you Loops, you have to stay in bed and follow my instructions or you will not make it," insisted Dr. Hoppins. "I'll take my leave now."

Loops turned to Floza, "Floza, listen to me. I am feeling much better," said Loops.

"Father please, you can barely walk, I have to stay here and take care of you," insisted Floza.

Loops was a very stubborn man; he also felt that by having his daughter care for him, it would mean he was a bad father. "But you have to attend school Floza, your examinations are coming up," he argued.

"Father, right now I am worried because you are the only person I have," and she broke down in tears. "Please let me just be here, until you are well. I promise that I will listen to you after you get better."

With not much of a choice, Loops agreed. That night as the clouds covered the moon, Floza looked out of her window, with Rods by her side. She gazed into the sky, wondering how this could have happened to her father.

To Floza, her father was a man of iron, and to see him in this condition was strange and frightening.

"Floza! Floza!" Someone had called her name. "I am here, down here, can you see me?"

It was none other than Edor.

"You again! What do you want from me?" yelled Floza. "Little girl, I don't want anything from you," slurred the panther. "I just stopped by to find out how your father is doing? I heard Mrs. Poppsy saying that he has come down with a virus."

"Since when are you so concerned about my father?" asked Floza.

"Since I have lived in Clobet Valley and since I know what is wrong with him," said Edor, in a sly voice.

"You have only been in Clobet Valley recently," replied Floza. "How could you possibly know what is wrong with my father?"

"Where I come from, what he is experiencing is very common. 'Virus IV258' is very common," said the panther.

"How would you know this?" asked Floza.

"Flo. I know more than you think," said the panther. "Now you and I both know that the cure for this virus is not in Clobet."

"My name is Floza thank you. Only my friends are allowed to call me Flo," said Floza angrily.

"Poor Dr. Hoppins, he is in a situation, he knows he does not have a cure," said Edor. "So he is just going to let your father die!"

"No cried Floza, you are lying. You are trying to trick me!"

"Now why would I trick you, little girl?" said Edor. "I just came to visit, because I have a solution. I can get you the cure, yes indeed. But you have to come with me, away from this place. You need to come with me to my world if you want to save your father."

"But I can't just leave him alone," said Floza.

"He will be fine," replied Edor. "I have a temporary solution. These are pills that will make him better, but only for a while." He held out his paw. "You see the virus will live in his body that is if he is not injected with the cure. So, in that time while he is well and breathing, you will come into my world and I will surely give you what you need."

"Why are you offering me help? I don't trust you one bit," asked Floza.

"You see little girl, your father and I have a debt to settle, this is the only reason. I can't give you more information, so the offer still stands. You can take the pills from my paw, or watch your father die a slow and miserable death."

Floza was extremely confused. She did not trust the cat one bit, but she also had no other alternative to save her father. There was no way that Doctor Hoppins could find a cure, and not in time to save her father.

"Alright, I accept your offer," said Floza.

"You will not regret this," replied Edor, handing over the pills to the girl. "I must take leave now, but be sure to meet me at the bridge at the lake before sunrise. Do not make a mistake as to trick me. I have my ways of finding out; don't be fooled by my animal appearance."

"No Edor, I will keep to my word," she promised, and of she went into the cottage.

CHAPTER 3

THE JOURNEY TO DURBEY

Later that night, Floza, after much anticipation, decided to give Loops the temporary cure.

"Floza, I have been searching for you, I needed my walking stick, it's just behind the door," said Loops.

"Yes father, I do apologize but Dr. Hoppins was just at the door", answered Floza.

"Really, and why did he decide to pay a visit at such a late hour?" asked Loops. "Well he did apologize, but he brought good news with him," replied Floza.

The little girl held out her hand, and in them was the temporary cure for Loops virus. Pretending to look glad about the temporary solution, Floza presented her father with the pills that would sustain his health until she could receive the original cure from Edor. She knew she had to contain the fear within her; she now had to venture out into another world with a mysterious cat whom she distrusts.

But after seeing the relief in her father's eyes she knew that her sacrifice would be worth it, after all Loops was the only family she had.

"A cure you say? I can't believe my ears, I thought this news would never come," said Loops.

"Hurry! Take them father, we must not wait till morning."

She handed Loops a glass of water and with tears in his eyes he gulped the temporary cure, the cure he thought would be permanent.

"Lies!" thought Floza, "I never had a reason to lie to father until now, but this is the only solution that has presented itself and from a talking cat. I will have to pack for tomorrow, I can't take much as it will be too obvious and father will think I ran away."

So she packed her little suitcase with a few clothes and a few pictures of her father and mother. Early that morning before the sun rose, she snuck out of her room. She looked in her father's room to check if he was fine. The color of his face clearly showed that the cure was working. With mixed feelings of relief and sadness, Floza left to meet Edor. She hurried to the bridge, which was situated close to the lake, where Edor had requested she meet him. As she got closer to the bridge saw Edor patiently awaiting her arrival.

"I thought you would never make it," said Edor. "Well I was taught by my father to keep to my word," replied Floza.

"If only he had kept to his word. Your father needs to practice what he preaches," said Edor.

"Whatever do you mean?" asked Floza.

"In time girl, you will finally understand what your father really is. We have to hurry now, the trip to Durbey is not an easy journey," he replied mysteriously.

"Durbey? What is Durbey?" asked Floza.

"Durbey is the world I was talking about," replied Edor.

"It's actually just a city in the big world that exists. You see Clobet is a very small place in a very big world." "I thought that Clobet was the only place that exists with humans," said Floza.

"Well you have a lot to learn little girl, a lot to learn," mumbled Edor. "Now run when I tell you to, I don't have all day to get you to Durbey."

They both managed to pass the guards when they were not looking. As they both walked down a hill, Edor asked Floza, "Have you ever teleported before?"

"Teleported?" asked Floza, "I have never heard off such a word."

"It is a mixture of magic and science, in fact it is the fastest way to travel," said Edor. "My very own scientists have invented the teleporting bubble; do you see this little ball?" The panther opened his paw and in it was a little ball.

"I am scared!" said Floza," I don't know what sorcery you are using, but I am not prepared to teleport to Durbey."

"Well, if you refuse to travel with the bubble, there is no other way to Durbey, and you will have to go back home. You do know what that means? Your father will die and it will be all your fault," said Edor.

"Okay I accept," said Floza, and as the bubble expanded, they both stepped inside.

"Close your eyes little girl, it's your first time travelling by bubble, it could make you feel a bit sick," warned Edor.

"Sick?" asked Floza, "I thought you said it was the best way to travel. But of course, you always sugar coat everything, it's your nature."

"Hold on! It's time to leave Clobet Valley," said Edor. "Goodbye Clobet Valley, I do hope I will come back home soon," thought Floza.

The bubble flew higher and higher. It was transparent just like a normal bubble but it seemed to be controlled by Edor with one of his devices that looked like a watch. As they travelled, they passed over fields and houses and huge farms.

"Look how beautiful the sight is!" said Edor. "But honestly it is not as beautiful as Durbey; you will see for yourself how splendid my city is. No, how spectacular my city is!" laughed Edor.

"Any other describing words you would like to use?" asked Floza in a condescending tone.

"Wow! You can be a cheeky girl!" said Edor. "And to think I was starting to like you. Its time," said Edor.

"Time for?" asked Floza.

"It's time for us to land. We have reached Durbey, Floza. Behold the city of Durbey", the panther replied.

It was beautiful. The city was colorful and the buildings were tall as if they were reaching for the sky and the lights were illuminating electric colors. Once the bubble landed it was time for Floza to step out into the new world; it was new and captivating to the eyes, nothing like Clobet Valley. One building stood out; it was the tallest building with a pointy roof and glass bricks.

"That is Hendo Enterprises. Isn't it beautiful?" said Edor as his eyes lit up, and he waved his long tail. "We must walk out of this park," said Edor. "This is Florence Gardens; it was the safest and most private place to land."

They both walked to the City where Floza found herself in a strange market place.

"Welcome to Durbey," said Edor, as he licked his paw.

Crowds of people walked by on the streets. They were dressed smartly in colorful coats and hats. There was music all around and entertainment on the streets. The vibe was magnificent. The train tracks were high up in between the buildings and the trains were state of the art and travelled at an exhilarating speed.

All of this was peculiar to Floza but she was amazed by this site; this world that she just entered was modern and so advanced.

"I cannot believe a place such as this exists," thought Floza. "Sure, I thought Edor was exaggerating when he boosted about Durbey. But now I see how beautiful this place really is, so much different from Clobet Valley. Still I must not forget the intention of my visit at Durbey. This is for father and as soon as I get the cure, I will leave this place."

"That's called a skyscraper dear," said Edor. "I am sure you understand why, you are a clever girl after all."

"Yes, I understand why Edor," she said, and as Floza looked around she realized that her longing to see outside Clobet Valley may have led Edor to her. But there is still a long way to go with this story and much for Floza to learn about Edor and her new-found home. "This is where I will leave you," said Edor.

"I'm sorry I did not get that Edor?" asked Floza.

"This is where I will leave you Floza," said Edor. "I will meet you at Florence Gardens tomorrow. For now, you are on your own."

"You must be joking Edor! How could you bring me here to this perfect-looking place and you promised me, you promised that you would give me the cure. I am just a girl! How can you leave me alone? I am fifteen years old Edor, how do you expect me to survive here alone in this strange new city?" asked Floza.

"I told you I would give you the cure but I did not promise that I would give you a place to stay and provide for you, you read me all wrong," replied Edor.

"But I am scared," said Floza, "Where will I live?"

"Here is some money, there is a women's hostel on 13th Street," said Edor. And he held out his paw with notes and coins.

"Money?" asked Floza? "What use does this have?" "It is the only thing you need to survive," said Edor,

"Without this you are nothing. So, I suggest you find yourself a job to get more of this money, until the cure is ready."

"But how long will the cure take?" asked Floza, "You told me that you already have the cure."

"I can't believe this is happening!" thought Floza, "I am all alone in this big crowded place. The people don't look pleasant, they glare at you. I think that lady was staring at my dress."

"I'll take my leave now, we will meet the day after tomorrow at Florence Gardens," said Edor.

"Okay." replied Floza with not much of a choice, "I will go to the women's hostel right away!" and off she went to find 13th Street.

"Selfish cat!" thought Floza, as she walked at a fast pace, as to avoid the people. "So, this is twelfth street, I am most definitely close." As Floza walked she tripped over something. It was a walking stick; it was a tall very stern looking man with a long trench coat walking down the street.

"Watch where you are walking girl," shouted the man.

"I am so sorry Sir," said Floza, frightened by the man's intruding presence. She ran as fast as she could, and as she ran, she thought of how she had ended up in this horrible situation. "But this is for Loops. He is the only person I have and I will not let him die," she thought.

As she walked in the streets of Durbey, Floza could not help noticing the unique style the people had. The clothes they wore were rather brightly colored. Women and men wore hats, but not just any hats, rather stylish hats with outstanding decorations. There was a vibe in the atmosphere, music was playing and people were dancing on the corner of the streets. The streets were filled with hotels, social scenes where people laughed and celebrated each other's company. This world was a total contrast from Clobet Valley.

She noticed a sign saying, 'Salisbury Hotel'. It was a rather large building made off glass. It was illuminated with lights; all the buildings were. It sure was a sight to see.

Floza walked into the hotel. There were crystal chandlers and the floors were made with glass tiles, the colors seemed to be changing as if there was lighting in the floors. An old-fashioned girl from a valley, in a glamorous city, how could Floza blend into this world?

Just as she was about to leave a women approached Floza; she wore a dazzling dress and the most captivating jewelery.

"Excuse me, you are?" asked the Lady.

"Hello Miss, my name is Floza, I am looking for a place to stay."

"You don't look like you can afford this place, this is the finest hotel in Durbey Town. Unless... you have six gold pieces hidden in that flimsy dress of yours? I doubt it!" and the lady laughed as she mocked Floza's appearance.

"Six gold pieces Miss? I have these ten silvers. Will this be enough for the night?" asked Floza.

"You're just a poor girl trying her luck, I see," said the lady. "You can't afford to stay here. Leave this hotel, you're making it look bad."

Floza was stunned by the woman's reaction; she was rather rude. Floza followed the women's instruction. She ran away from the hotel as fast as she could, and as she ran, she saw a women's hostel, 'Eva's Women's Home'. She ran up the flight of stairs and stopped at the reception.

"Slow down, no running! Did you not see the sign?" said a women sitting behind a desk. She was thin with red hair and wore funny looking spectacles. Her nose was rather long and she had the most perfect posture.

"I'm sorry," said Floza gasping for air.

"What do you want here?" asked the Lady.

"May I know your name?" asked Floza.

"Grace! Some call me Gracy. Are you looking for accommodation?" Gracy enquired.

"Why yes Miss, I would like a place to stay," replied Floza. And she held out the money Edor had given her. "We do have a bed available, that would be five silvers for the night," said the woman.

"Thanks Miss," replied Floza as she smiled contently at Grace.

"Just a warning little girl!" the woman said. "You may call me Floza," Floza smiled.

"Well then Floza, the women can get rather catty at times. So best to keep your space, dinner will be served at six o clock sharp. I will show you to your bed, do you have any belongings you would like me to lock away?" asked Grace.

"No Miss, I don't have anything with me."

"And clothes?" asked Grace. "What will you wear tomorrow?"

Floza watched her snarling at her as if she committed a huge crime.

"Okay then, there is a store down the road called Pebbles. You can get some decent clothes there and at a decent price. Just remember girl, you or any other women living in this hostel are not permitted to leave after seven o clock, is that clear?" said the women.

"Yes Miss, clear as crystal," replied Floza.

They reached a hallway that was rather long and as they walked further down, they passed many rooms, and in the rooms were a number of beds. There must have been about twenty rooms; it was a very big hostel and was very neat and tidy.

"This is your room," said Grace, as she introduced the girl to her bed. It was not actually her room; it was occupied with a number of beds. But it was a bed and shelter for the night.

A number of women of all shapes and sizes flocked in, yapping and laughing loudly. Many of the ladies worked and would just come home in time for dinner.

"Ladies! Attention!" yelled Grace. "This is your new roommate, what's your name again girl?"

"Floza", she replied.

"This is Floza!" Grace had a very high-pitched voice that echoed through the hallway. Oh, hello, they did not seem to be friendly and then pretended she was not there.

"The kitty litter is in the small room over there." Grace pointed to a little room in the corner.

"Kitty Litter?" asked Floza, looking confused at Grace. "Yes, yes, I have to go now. I am very busy," and she huddled out of the room ignoring her question.

"What ever would I need kitty litter for? I'm not a cat," thought Floza.

"What animal are you?" snorted a fat looking girl with two pig tales. "My name is Stacy, and you are?"

"Pleased to meet you. My name is Floza. I beg your pardon, I am a little confused as I thought you asked me about me being an animal," said Floza.

"Yes, we all have some aspect of animal to us, so what animal are you?" asked Stacy.

"I have never thought about it, I would not compare animals and human beings. They are totally different," replied Floza.

"Quite the contrary," said Stacy as she nodded her head. A siren rang and the women raced from their rooms to the dining hall.

"I'll walk you there," said Stacy.

"Thanks very much," said Floza. She was rather relieved. After all, Grace had mentioned all the women were catty. Stacy seemed friendly although a bit peculiar.

"So why are you here?" asked Stacy.

"Well, I am here on vacation," replied Floza. "I am here to visit my uncle, and you?"

"Well, my parents passed away a month back. They were attacked by a wolf," said Stacy.

Floza looked at her surprised. "That is very unfortunate."

"Wolves are a cat's worst enemy, not many live in these parts," said Stacy. "But unfortunately, my parents were out at night and well, in the wrong place at the wrong time."

"I have learnt about wolves in Zoology class, we don't have wolves at Clobet Valley, although I did see a panther once and he is rather prudish," said Floza.

"Clobet, haven't heard of that place before," snarled Stacy.

"It is in the countryside," replied Floza.

They reached the hall, it was very big, with a high ceiling and long tables occupying the entire hall. As they got closer, she heard meowing and purring, what sounded like cats.

"We are here," said Stacy, "Dinner smells good!" and she licked her lips.

Floza followed Stacy to the hall and when they entered something really strange caught her eyes. There were cats, cats everywhere; they were seated on chairs and eating from plates filled with what looked like fish tails and other parts.

These cats were in fact cat people, they were furry and walked on two legs. Although there were different types of cat people, fat cats, Persian cats, tom cats, more and more cats.

"Oh, my goodness! We are in the wrong room! What are these cats doing here," yelled Floza and to her amazement Stacy transformed into a brown chubby cat, with a short tail which quite resembled her stubby physique. Stacy pounced up onto the dining table, to get her share of dinner.

"What are you waiting for?" asked Stacy. "It is time to eat."

"But, but," said Floza, "I am not hungry," and she left for bed. She could not understand what had happened to the women.

Floza did not think that Grace meant the women were catty in a figurative manner. "Things are getting stranger and stranger," she thought.

"I need to get some sleep and when I wake up in the morning, this will all make sense." So Floza went off to bed, she closed her eyes and tried to pretend it was all a bad dream.

The next morning Floza woke to the yelling of young women around her bed. One of the women in the hostel had apparently stolen a ball of wool from one of the other ladies.

"It's mine! How would you accidently find a ball of wool that happened to belong to me under your bed?" yelled the woman. The woman accused, or should I say cat accused, was a lanky young lady who looked as if she was about to burst into tears.

"I am very sorry, please forgive me, but don't accuse me of stealing," replied the woman. Her name was Sara and she was not from those parts, she lived in a city called Galley town, where only tomcats lived.

"I can't deal with this yapping," said Floza as she pulled the sheets aside to get out of bed.

There was no sign of Stacy and it was time for breakfast.

"I can't believe what an awful dream I had last night," thought Floza. "It is definitely home sicknesses. I miss Father and Rods. Father will be so worried, I just vanished but this is for him, he will understand and I promise to tell him the whole story when I get back."

She got ready for breakfast and walked to the dining hall. She stepped into the hall, amazed as ever that there were women sitting at the dining table enjoying their breakfast. Stacy popped up and said:

"Welcome officially to breakfast, you will definitely enjoy this morning's oatmeal. Floza, why do you look so surprised, like you have seen a ghost?"

"Well, I had a bad dream last night about the dining hall filled with cats, and you were…" she paused, "A cat as well."

"How horrible," replied Stacy. "Yes indeed," said Floza.

"How horrible, because I am a cat," said Stacy. "Do you not recall me mentioning we all have an animal aspect to us? It only happens at six o clock."

"What happens?" asked Floza.

"The cat transformation," giggled Stacy, "But we transform back into our human selves every morning at six o clock. Floza was stunned and confused at the same time. She could not believe what she was hearing. What was this world where human and animals live?

"So Stacy, are all the people of Durbey cat people?" asked Floza.

"No there are normal people like you," replied Stacy, and she changed the topic to avoid answering the question.

"Clobet Valley is so different from this world" thought Floza. "I don't know anyone properly from this place, more importantly who do I trust? Can I trust Edor to keep to his promise about father's cure? He did mention that he knows of a secret regarding father. I am going to drive myself crazy if I do not occupy myself today. I am meeting Edor tomorrow at Florence Gardens and he will have to give me answers. I hope I remember how to get there…. I will have to stop and ask for directions." She sat down next to Stacy to have breakfast. She noticed a newspaper lying on the dining table next to one of the women.

"Good Morning, may I please have a look at the newspaper, I promise I won't be long," asked Floza.

"Sure," said the lady without hesitation.

What captivated her the most was the front-page story. It stated:

Our City Billionaire Mr. Hendo Wallens will be a judge for the talent show at the Annual Durbey Fair.

She noticed the picture of a studious looking man, tall with a top hat and long trench coat. He was holding the bubble teleporter, the very same teleporter the panther had used.

She read further to find out what the hype was about. It was mostly about the annual Durbey fair and a brief description of the teleporting bubble. It stated in the newspaper that it was designed by Mr. Hendo and had the ability of transporting him to any part of the world and not limited to, but also other galaxies.

"Edor was using this man's invention and is not that smart after all," thought Floza. She finished off her breakfast and got ready for her day out at Durbey City.

As she left the women's hostel, Grace approached her.

"I do hope you are enjoying your stay Floza, I hope the women's cattiness did not get to you much. I did not get to see you at dinner, in fact I am always busy. I don't have time for dinner, managing the hostel is a tricky business."

"Yes Gracy, I am actually going to visit the store, to get some clothes at Pebbles," said Floza with a confused expression on her face hoping she got the name correct.

"You mentioned it yesterday?"

"Yes Pebbles, do enjoy," said Grace.

"I will thank you Gracy," replied Floza.

As she walked into the crowded city as ever, she noticed that everyone was always in a hurry.

"I miss the laid back quietness of Clobet Valley," thought Floza.

She reached Pebbles Store. She noticed some lovely clothes and tried some on. She soon decided she would take the yellow dress and a blouse for the skirt she was already wearing. As she reached the counter, there was a posh looking women chatting to the person at the counter. She could not help over hearing their conversation, after all they spoke so loudly. The subject of their conversation was about how the billionaire scientist Mr. Hendo is searching for new recruits to work at Hendo Enterprises. As she left the store, she could not help wondering why this man Mr. Hendo Wallens was so famous and powerful.

As she walked back to the women's hostel, she noticed a sign outside one of the stores. It was actually a restaurant.

"Res-tau-rant," read Floza. "What is a restaurant?" The sign stated workers were needed.

Since she needed a job, she decided to go into the restaurant to find out more. The restaurant was called 'Eat your heart out'.

"Sounds very brutal," thought Floza. But she needed a job urgently to pay for her hostel fee, so she walked in and rung the counter bell.

Out wobbled a fat man with an angry face. He wore his pants to the waist and his shirt was held tightly with a pair of braces.

The man leaned over the counter, lifting his head up he said to Floza,

"How can I help you? Take a look at our Sunday specials."

"No Sir, actually I noticed the sign outside and I want to work here, as a waitress," replied Floza. She did not even know what a waitress was but she needed anything she could get.

"Is that so?" replied the man. "I am Charlie the owner of this fine restaurant. Tell me girl, how many years of experience in waitressing do you have?"

Mr. Charlie was a very proud man; he took pride in managing his restaurant that had been passed down through the family for generations.

Floza paused for an instant. "None at all Sir. I don't have any experience in waitressing. But I am a quick learner. I often helped out at our Annual Fair and I don't feel nervous around people."

"Well that is quite obvious, after all you are a minor, and how old are you girl?"

"I am fifteen," replied Floza.

"So, you are underage then, I am not allowed to employ children. It is against the law," said the man.

"Well then thank you for your time Sir, I will leave." "Wait!" said Mr. Charlie. "I don't know why, but I feel

sorry for you. I may have a position available for you. But you are not permitted to come out into the dining area, it's too risky."

A sudden glow filled Floza's face, her pale face suddenly looked as red as a radish. It had been a long time since she had felt a sense of satisfaction. "Why thank you Sir, I accept your offer," replied the excited girl.

"Good. You start tomorrow, be here at seven am sharp," said Mr. Charlie.

"Thanks again Mr. Charlie," said Floza. And the girl hurried off to meet Edor at Florence Gardens.

CHAPTER 4

FLORENCE GARDENS

"Finally, something has gone right for once!" thought Floza. "I am so relieved that I have found a job just in time to pay my hostel fee."

As she walked down the street, she noticed a sign reading Florence Gardens. It was a busy garden, filled with pink roses and daisies. At the entrance of the garden was a big gate. It was gold in color with the name 'Florence Gardens' engraved on it. Floza walked through the garden and as she did, she saw families of Durbey riding bicycles and having picnics.

"What a beautiful sight," thought Floza. "This reminds me of Mrs. Poppsy's garden. For a moment, it feels like I am home. I miss Father so very much."

"Father would be so worried!" thought Floza. "He would think that I ran away because he is a bad father. I have to get the cure for Fathers illness soon, before I get lost in this world."

Floza walked through Florence Gardens; she thought of all the questions she had needed to ask Edor. After all, so many strange things had happened at Durbey. She had not expected to be living in a hostel full of cats, nor did she expect to be in a strange world on her own.

"I am sure Edor will be on time," thought Floza. "He is a very meticulous panther." Floza noticed children playing merrily with their parents. This made her think of her family and how she wished her mother was alive.

"Things would have been perfect," thought Floza, "Why if mother were around, she would know what to do in these situations." "Father is all I have now, and I will do everything in my power, to get him the cure," thought Floza.

After some time, she noticed in the distance Edor standing next to what looked like a stand of balloons. Balloons of all colors. He was handing them out to children who passed by with their families. But what was the occasion? She walked steadily towards Edor as to confront him about his peculiar action.

"So, I see you have made it to Florence Gardens in one piece," said Edor. "I was wondering if you would actually meet me. After all, you are ten minutes late, you do know I don't like waiting," said the panther. He was very annoyed as he hated waiting.

"What color balloon do you want girl?" asked Edor. "None for me thank you," replied Floza.

"It's a very special day," said Edor. "Special day?" asked Floza.

"Yes! Today is the day I finally get to see an old friend of mine," smiled Edor.

"That's good," said Floza. She was very uninterested in this friend Edor mentioned.

"I have actually found a job thank you for asking", said Floza trying to sound condescending. "Please tell me Edor when will I receive the cure?"

"It should not take me more than a week girl. Until then continue to blend in as you are doing," replied Edor. "How do you expect me to blend in? You failed to tell me that the people of Durbey are in fact cat people," said Floza angrily.

"Yes, yes, I forgot to mention this one thing," replied Edor.

"But I felt it was not important. In fact, not all people of Clobet are cats. You see the women's hostel you are living at houses a different species of human that have existed since evolution."

"Most of these people experience symptoms of animal instincts and behavior from a very young age and eventually at their prime age the transformation process takes place. It is a secret race that has existed for years, the cats you live with, or shall I say cat people, are homeless beings from all parts of the world. They were expecting you after we landed in Durbey town."

"Expecting me how?" asked Floza. "That's impossible! How could they know that I would choose their hostel to live in?"

"Because I know how you think girl, you would choose the first hostel you came across," replied Edor. "But this is not important, what is important is that you save your dearest father Loops."

"I will definitely save my dearest father," replied Floza. "But first you need to answer my questions truthfully. Who are you really, and what do you know of my father?" She had rehearsed this question in her mind over and over again, hoping to not forget these lines. Floza knew that Edor had been hiding something and she needed to find out soon what it was.

"I can answer the first but the later will have to wait," said Edor whilst licking his paw.

"Don't worry little girl, your father will know by now that you have abandoned him to come to Durbey to live the dream you so desired."

"Whatever are you talking about, you know of fathers situation. He is the only reason I am here," said Floza.

"You cannot deny your deepest desire was to see outside of Clobet Valley. Your dream is now fur filled, no pun intended!" said Edor and he laughed maliciously.

"Please get to the point Edor. When will you give me father's cure? Will you keep to your word Edor?" begged Floza.

"Yes, I keep to my word," said the panther.

"I will take my leave now," said Floza, "I have work in the morning."

"We will meet again," said Edor, "I will send you a message for our next meeting."

"That is fine but how will you send me this message?" asked Floza.

"I mean how will we communicate?"

"I will write to you or send you a message when the time comes," replied Edor, and he vanished into thin air.

"Must be his teleporting device," thought Floza.

"I have a feeling Edor is up to no good, like he is conspiring something. I am not certain what he is conspiring but I shall find out soon. The Durbey Fair is in a few days; I will have a chance to meet other people from Durbey. I am sure someone will know who Edor really is."

Later that day Floza went back to the women's hostel, for dinner. Some of the lady cats were ranting and raving about the annual Durbey fair.

"I can't wait!" said Sara. "I would love to go for a ride on the Ferris Wheel!" and she meowed as to get her other cat friends to agree.

The lady cats at the hostel did not go out very often and so looked forward to the annual Durbey Fair. The Durbey Fair was quite a spectacular event filled with color, music and all sorts of exciting games.

"I am sure it is nothing like our Clobet Fair," thought Floza. Clobet Valley had a beautiful fair every summer, it would attract merchants and traders and the people of Clobet played games of all sorts. One special event was the Clobet posh pets competition were people would dress their dogs and cats in little outfits.

Mrs. Poppsy was responsible for running this competition; she was very experienced with pets and the town mayor was adamant that she was the best suited person to judge the event.

"I will not be able to attend this year's fair," thought Floza.

"Father will be all alone this year. He will have to run the stall by himself." Loops and Floza also participated in the Clobet Fair, they would sell potted plants and fertilizers as Loops had always taken a liking to gardening. Floza naturally enjoyed this as she always assisted her father with the garden. Floza thought about how special her father was to her and she believed that although he would be upset with her. She had no choice because after all he had a fatal illness and his life was in her hands.

"Since I cannot attend the fair at Clobet I will try my best to help Stacy with her stall," she thought.

"Come to think of it I have not seen Stacy today, I wonder where she could be? it's almost dinner time."

Floza was quite fond of Stacy. She was the only friend she had at Durbey. Although she was quite direct at times as she always spoke her mind. Just as Floza was about to go to the dining hall, Stacy walked into the room. She seemed very upset, like she had been crying. It was quite unusual to see her in this mood as she was always cheerful.

"What is the matter Stacy?" asked Floza.

"It's nothing, replied Stacy. I just had a long day at work, we had a lot of cake orders. At this time of the year everyone in Durbey are so cheerful. There are weddings and all sorts of happy occasions."

Stacy was a baker. She worked for Mr. Stevens who was the owner of a bakery called 'The Cherry on Top'. He was always such a difficult man, an absolute perfectionist that took pride in all his cakes. If the slightest decoration was out of line, he would request that the cake be thrown away.

"I am sorry," said Floza, "I don't know how my boss will treat me but I need this job desperately."

"Boss?" asked Stacy she had a confused expression on her face.

"I found a job today," replied Floza, "At a restaurant. It is called 'Eat your heart out'." Floza couldn't pronounce restaurant, she had not even known what a restaurant was before she had come to Durbey.

"Oh! I have eaten there before!" said Stacy. She had an unpleasant look on her face like it was not the best place to be.

"You don't seem very happy about my new job," asked Floza.

"Is there something you would like to perhaps tell me Stacy?"

"Ummm well," said Stacy, "It's just the owner Mr. Charles." Stacy seemed hesitant to reply to Floza's question.

"But why, did she know something perhaps a secret about the restaurant?"

"You mean Mr. Charlie" said Floza, "I have met him already. He seems very strict but you don't have to worry about me Stacy. I will be fine," said Floza as she patted her hand on Stacy's shoulder.

"It's just Floza, there were rumors about Mr. Charlie, about him selling his wife as a slave," said Stacy.

"What on earth are you talking about?" asked Floza. She thought this was just a bizarre story and obviously thought it sounded ridiculous.

"Well, Mr. Charlie was on the verge of losing his restaurant, due to not having enough money, until he did a major turnaround. The funny thing is that his wife disappeared and some say he traded her as a slave to Mr. Hendo the wealthiest man in Durbey. Floza, once you become a worker for Mr. Hendo well you become bound by a lifelong contract which cannot be broken. Some say Mr. Hendo bewitches the contract with all sorts of magic and spells which he likes to call science," replied Stacy.

"All these words sound so foreign to me," replied Floza, looking confusingly at Stacy. "I am sure those are just rumors.

"Don't be silly Stacy. Why on earth would Mr. Charlie sell his wife to another man?"

"No, no Floza. It's not just another man, this man is Mr. Hendo Wallens, the most powerful man in Durbey, owner of many multinational corporations and famous scientist," said Stacy.

Floza thought that this name sounded familiar. She had seen it in the newspaper and overheard a lady at Pebbles talk about him.

"Pebbles? Really? You have been there?" asked Stacy. "Well yes," said Floza, "I needed a few clothes. Come on, let's go to our rooms. I can't wait to show you the new dress I bought." When Floza put the dress on and Stacy told her how lovely she looked. She thought it looked like a dress a ballerina would wear.

"It sure does," said Floza, "In fact can you keep a secret Stacy? I actually go for ballet practice at Clobet Valley, ballet which is quite popular."

"That sounds marvelous!" said Stacy. Of course I will keep your secret. I wish I could dance but my physique won't allow me to move gracefully."

"That's not funny," said Floza. "I am sure you would make a great ballerina."

"I doubt it," said Stacy. "Floza, I have an idea. Why don't you take part in the Durbey Talent Show?"

"No, I couldn't," replied Floza. "I am not a professional ballet dancer."

"Oh, don't be silly Flo, I am sure with a bit of practice you will be the best performer at the talent show," answered Stacy.

"How would you know Stacy?" You have not seen me dance! I could be really bad," warned Floza.

Stacy suggested that Floza show her the dance the next day. She said she would ask Gracy for her radio and it would be perfect. Floza said that that should be fine but she couldn't promise that she would take part in the talent show.

"The one thing I forgot to mention is that Mr. Hendo Wallens himself will be judging the show along other famous singers and performers," said Stacy.

"Okay. Well, at least that will give me a chance to meet Thee Mr. Hendo Wallens," said Floza.

"Trust me Floza. It will be an absolute privilege to meet the most powerful man in Durbey."

"I enjoy Stacy's company," thought Floza, "but I cannot say too much to her or my plan to save father will fail. The only thing I can do is to keep this to myself."

"You seem deep in thought," said Stacy, "But trust me, this will be an awesome experience."

"What will you do at the Durbey Fair?" asked Floza.

"Well I am planning on selling toffee apples. I make them myself," said Stacy.

"I love toffee apples! Mrs. Poppsy makes them for the Clobet Fair, so delicious," said Floza.

"Mrs. Poppsy?" asked Stacy?

"Yes Mrs. Poppsy. Why do you ask?" Floza said.

"That name sounds familiar," replied Stacy. "I have heard it somewhere."

"You might have heard it somewhere. It is not a very common name, but I am sure someone in Durbey also has that name," replied Floza.

"Floza I hope you will reconsider working for Mr. Charlie, I would hate to see you hurt," said Stacy.

"I appreciate your concern Stacy. I would do the same for you, however I need this job to pay for my hostel fee and I can assure you I will be fine," replied Floza.

"Floza, you have never mentioned your father before, which part of Durbey does he live in?" asked Stacy.

"Well Stacy my father lives outside the City of Durbey in the hills."

"The hills? I have not seen this place," replied Stacy. "Yes, not many have." said Floza.

Floza did not want to lie to Stacy, but she had not much of a choice after all Stacy would not understand anything about Clobet Valley. It was time for dinner and both the girls got ready to go to the dining hall. This time Floza made a special request for dinner; she did not want to eat the food the chef had prepared for the cat ladies.

"This smells good!!" said Stacy.

"What on earth is that?" asked Floza.

"It is one of my favorites, fish tail soup!! One of Chefs best dishes!! It's the best fish tail soup I have eaten since …"

"Since?" questioned Floza.

"Since my mother made it" replied Stacy. "The last time I saw my mother, this was the last dish she prepared for me.

Not that it was her favorite dish too, she did not enjoy the cat dishes."

"Why not Stacy?" asked Floza.

"Well mmmm.... my mother was not a cat Floza. Actually, I mean, my mother could not transform into a cat!!"

"Is that why you are half human?" asked Floza.

"No no," said Stacy "I am not half human nor am I half cat. It's a transformation process that takes place."

"I know... at six in the evening and you turn back to human form at six in the morning. Is it a painful process, I mean the transformation?" questioned Floza. "Umm, not actually," said Stacy, "It's not something that I enjoy. Being covered in fur is not very comfortable. And well, my senses change, my hearing gets louder, I can't listen to music much, at least not loudly. So Floza, there are limitations to being a cat, except for one."

"Except for one? Which one?" asked Floza.

"Never mind," said Stacy, "It's time for dessert!! Wait a minute! Where is your dinner Floza?" "How rude of me! All this time I was gobbling my food I didn't realize you were not eating."

"I am having baked potatoes and fish on the side," said Floza. "The chef will prepare this for me since I am not very fond of fish tale soup. I am trying to get her attention before she rushes off into the kitchen. Chef, Chef Prudence!"

"Yes child? No need to yell, your dinner is almost ready," said the chef.

Chef Prudence was a chubby lady, with a big face, who always wore her cooking hat and apron. She waddled over to Floza, to give her the meal she ordered.

"There you go, now enjoy young lady," said the Chef. "Thank you Chef Prudence," said Floza as she smiled with contentment.

"Chef Prudence never fails to make a delicious meal."

"No she doesn't," replied Stacy, gobbling her food. "I love absolutely everything she prepares!"

"You mean you absolutely love food," said Floza.

"You do know me really well Floza," Stacy replied.

Both the girls giggled over dinner and soon after called it a night.

CHAPTER 5

THE MEETING

Floza's disappearance was a shock to the whole town; the people of Clobet made up a number of bizarre stories about her disappearance. One story made up by Little Jim was quite strange. He told all the children in school that Floza had been kidnapped by a strange man that lived in the hills, who ate children.

Many of the children believed this and so refused to go near the hills. When their parents had asked why they were afraid, they blurted out about little Jim's story. Another story that was quite strange was made up by an old lady in Clobet Town. She told all her customers that Floza had run away to look for her husband in another country. This sounded ridiculous to everyone as Floza was just a teenager, marriage was far from her mind.

"I just cannot wrap my finger around my little Floza's disappearance," thought Loops.

"I know I was not much for her and I tried my best to raise her my best, but I always knew it was not enough for her."

"Still I know she would not have run away from me, after all were would she go? She does not know of any family beyond Clobet Valley. I just want my daughter back in one peace."

Loops heard a knock on the front door.

He wondered who this could be, and when he opened the door it was none other than Rods, trying to make his way into the house.

"Rods! I know you miss Floza dearly," said Loops. Rods signed as if he understood what Loops had said, he had missed her a lot and would at times go to her room after school and look for her, only to find the room was empty and Floza was not there anymore.

"I shall take you for a walk in the valley tomorrow, I think we could both do good with a bit of fresh air," said Loops.

It was one week since Floza's disappearance, and the elders gathered together at the town's school hall to address Floza's mysterious disappearance. The elders who attended the meeting were none other than Mrs. Poppsy, Headmaster Mr. Nimble, Suzy's Grandfather Dr. Hoppins, the town cobbler Mr. Thimble and not forgetting Loops.

Since Loops was in no state to chair the meeting, which he usually did, Mrs. Poppsy decided to fill his role. Ever since Floza had disappeared, Loops could not eat or sleep. He often rehearsed in his mind the last time Floza had spoken to him, the time she had given him the pills to sustain his illness, but of course he did not know this was from Edor.

"Floza my dearest child where would you have gone?" thought Loops.

"Did you perhaps run away because I was not a good father?"

"I tried to discipline you for your own good, but maybe I was too hard on you." Loops recalled the last incident, which left a negative mark in his mind, the time when he had shouted at Floza for frightening all the children at school about the panther. Little did he know that Floza had just told him the truth. It was a moment Loops felt guilty about, disciplining Floza a few nights before her disappearance.

"If you ever come back, I promise to be a better parent, the parent you deserve," thought Loops.

Loops sobbed every night before he went to bed, however he tried to put on a straight face to the people of Clobet. It was in fact Mrs. Poppsy's idea to meet, she felt it was time to address the disappearance of Floza and not forgetting her dearest Popsicle.

"My dear friends we are meeting today to discuss a very important matter," said Mrs. Poppsy.

"As we all know Floza has disappeared from the valley – it has been two weeks since her disappearance. We have sent out search parties from the swamp to the borders of the Valley, and since then we have received no indication of where Floza has gone. Not forgetting my dear Popsicle. He disappeared around about the same time as our Floza."

"It was just that night I read him his favorite bed time story about the dwarves who lived in the spooky forest. He loved that story. I cannot understand, why my Popsicle would run away from me," said Mrs. Poppsy.

Mrs. Poppsy was equally upset about Floza's disappearance; she had known Floza since she was a little girl, so did the other elders.

This surely was not an easy time for the elders of Clobet Valley. It had been sometime since Mrs. Poppsy had been so upset; the last time she had felt this devastated was when she had separated from her husband. Some said he had left her for another woman, others mentioned she had made stories about her separation to save her from embarrassment.

The elders of Clobet Valley were a close circle of friends who had shared many years together, way before the Valley was discovered. This is the reason all the friends stood together in unity, their relationship was more like family.

"I have informed the heads from neighboring areas to keep a look out for Floza," said Headmaster Nimble. "I am certain someone must have seen her leave the valley; we just have to try until we receive information about her whereabouts."

"Thank you! Nimble," said Mrs. Poppsy. "It is indeed a mystery, as to where young Floza has gone. I would have thought after Loops falling ill, she would at least stay by his side."

"Mrs. Poppsy, are you implying that Floza has run away from Clobet Valley?" asked Dr. Hoppins.

"No that is not what I am implying, Hoppins," replied Mrs. Poppsy as she shook her head so as to deny his statement.

"Errr, I really don't think we should be jumping to conclusions without the facts," said Mr. Thimble as he took of his coat, the room felt a bit too warm.

It was a very sensitive topic of discussion: you can imagine the confused expressions on everyone's face. At this point the elders did not have much evidence of Floza's disappearance, most of the discussion was based on assumptions.

It was the fear of the unknown that creeped into each and every elder's mind. Floza's mysterious disappearance was a difficult incident to comprehend, since there were so few clues.

"Loops. Would you like to add anything to this investigation?" asked Mr. Thimble.

"Well...not really..." replied Loops. He then paused as he was overwhelmed with discussing the disappearance of his dear Floza.

"Although I must say I feel glad to have friends such as yourselves. We have been through much more, but nothing can compare to the extent of loss I feel at this very moment. I just cannot understand, everything happened so fast, that night Floza had given me the cure that you recommended, Dr. Hoppins. I felt better immediately, and I was so grateful to you, and Floza, for restoring me to my health again."

"Cure? Whatever do you mean Loops?" asked Dr. Hoppins. "I did not present a cure to Floza, I did mention to her that it would take some time for me to discover the type of virus."

The elders looked at each other, in awe. The friends could not believe their ears. Why, if the cure was not from Dr. Hoppins, who was it from? The mystery behind Floza's disappearance had just become much more complex. There were no clues as to who had presented the cure to Floza.

"You cannot be serious," replied Loops, waving his hands to the side. "It was Floza who gave me the cure, she told me that it would make me better. She clearly mentioned it was from you, doctor. The night before her disappearance, Floza said that you visited our home and dropped off the cure. While you stood at the door, Floza mentioned that you were too busy to come into our home, and so you entrusted her to give me the cure."

"I can assure you Loops, I did not present any sort of pills to Floza," replied Dr. Hoppins, raising his eyebrows with certainty.

"Then who was Floza speaking to that night?" asked Mrs. Poppsy. There is no one other than doctor Hoppins who has the ability to find a cure, and in time.

"This makes no sense to me, there seems to be a missing link to the disappearance of Floza," said Dr. Hoppins as he scratched his head.

"It is quite strange that both Floza and Popsicle disappeared on the same night. Maybe there is some sort of relationship between these disappearances? We must look for clues," said Mr. Thimble.

"Funnily enough I saw Popsicle the night before his disappearance," said Mrs. Poppsy. I tucked him too bed and he was sound asleep, only to find the next morning his blanket turned over and his bed completely empty. I searched around the garden, and in the cottage, in every possible space Popsicle could have fitted."

"So Loops had seen Floza the night before her disappearance and you had seen Popsicle, that means, they both have disappeared during the early hours of the morning," replied Mr. Thimble.

"Early hours of the morning?" asked Dr. Hoppins but that would mean it was planned and perhaps the girl ran away.

"Why on earth would she take my precious Popsicle with her?" asked Mrs. Poppsy, trying to hold her tears back.

"After all, Floza was not very fond of cats, we all know that she was also not fond of Popsicle."

"Mrs. Poppsy you are being unfair to our friend Loops, we understand your feelings of sadness and I presume, loneliness since Popsicle's disappearance. However, the reason for our meeting is too address Floza's disappearance," replied Dr. Hoppins.

"Hoppins! Are you implying that Popsicle was not as important as Floza?" asked Mrs. Poppsy.

"No of course, that is not what I am implying. I meant that finding Floza is a priority, something tells me that both these disappearances are linked; once we solve Floza's disappearance, we shall find Popsicle."

"I agree!" replied Loops.

"Friends, we have not faced such problems since we moved to Clobet Valley. Our intention was to build a place that was safe from the outside world, a place away from our past," said Loops.

"Yes," replied Mrs. Poppsy, "I sometimes recall our lives before we came to Clobet Valley, and how perfect things were, when my husband and I were planning to have children. It almost came true, until......that wicked man entered our lives. I thought my husband would have followed me," sobbed Mrs. Poppsy. "Instead he decided his priority was his business, and becoming famous to the whole city."

"I...feel for you," said Headmaster Nimble. "We all left behind precious parts of our lives before we discovered Clobet Valley. Our families and the people of Clobet will never understand the hardships that were faced before Clobet Valley. Without those hardships we would have not discovered this life of equality amongst people, our children would not have survived the life we did."

"I agree," said Mr. Thimble. "We could only make the change – leaving that place behind was the best choice we made. I sometimes wonder how my mother is doing, I never got to say goodbye to her and it plays on my mind every day, however we pledged no contact with the outside world since any form of communication could lead him to us."

Mr. Thimble had not spoken to his mother since he moved to Clobet Valley; he had had to leave his mother behind. She would not have agreed with him leaving the city.

"Well know this, it does not help to talk about our past," said Headmaster Nimble, trying not to engage in this topic.

"It's a bit too late for that," said Loops, "We have already unpacked our emotions and feelings about the past. We now need to move forward, I am positive that we can solve the mystery of Floza's disappearance, and not forgetting Popsicle. Doctor, please find out if you can recall any clues from the night Floza was last seen. I will do the same. Mrs. Poppsy and Nimble, communicate to the people of Clobet regarding Floza's disappearance; it must be all over the Valley. We cannot keep this a secret, we are no longer safe at Clobet Valley.

"What about me?" asked Mr. Thimble. "How do I assist?"

"Thimble... my dear friend. I have a special task for you," said Loops as he whispered in Thimble's ear.

So the elders parted ways from the Town Hall, each playing a role in the investigation of Floza's disappearance. Although Mr. Thimbles role still remained a secret between himself and Loops, it must have been a very important task.

CHAPTER 6

WHEN DUTY CALLS

Meanwhile in Durbey Floza was getting ready to start her first day at 'Eat Your Heart Out'. She felt very nervous as this was her first job, after all she was just a little girl. Mr. Charlie had been kind enough to employ her as a dish-washer at his fine restaurant provided she did not communicate with the customers.

Mr. Charlie warned Floza of the consequences should she be seen at the dining area. It was a warm day and Floza decided to wear her new skirt that she had bought from

Pebbles clothing store. She was now ready for her first day at her new job. Floza joined the lady cats for breakfast in the dining hall. Stacy was at the dinner table enjoying fresh scones and croissants the cook had prepared for the morning breakfast.

"Would you like some croissants?" asked Stacy. "You'd better get them now before I gobble them up!" She laughed as if what she had just said was hilarious. Floza did not find it funny; after all she never got to eat properly at the hostel when Stacy was around.

"Why are you all dressed up Floza?" asked Stacy.

"Well Stacy, I thought you had remembered today is my first day at 'Eat Your Heart Out'," replied Floza. "Wish me luck will you Stacy?"

"Good luck!" replied Stacy, "You are going to need it, since Mr. Charlie is such a difficult man."

"I think I can handle Mr. Charlie, but thank you for being so concerned about me Stacy."

"I wonder why everyone is over-emphasizing the fact that Mr. Charlie is such a bad man; he gave me a job after all, can he be as bad as they say?"

"I'll soon find out," thought Floza, "I'm new at this work thing, and I know I will be just fine. Stacy I'll take leave now."

"Are you leaving so soon?" asked Stacy.

"Well yes. I have to start at seven o'clock considering I have to walk there. I would like not to disappoint Mr. Charlie on my first day," replied Floza.

"I am sure you won't," replied Stacy, with full faith that Floza would arrive to work on time. Floza left the Woman's hostel; she had to walk three streets to get to the restaurant. She passed Fifth Street, Sixth Street, Seventh Street; you don't have to guess which street she was on now.

She finally made it to Eighth Street to the restaurant 'Eat Your Heart Out'. Thank goodness I arrived here on time she thought. She was very relieved that she had made it on time, it was her first day and she wanted to make a good impression. In the dining area was Mr. Charlie. He was rather chubby and always wore an apron which read 'Come dine with us to your hearts content'. The restaurant was beautifully decorated with coordinated décor and the smell of pies lingered in the air.

The smell of pies reminded her so much of Mrs.

Poppsy's baked pies; it smelt so good and inviting.

"Welcome girl," said Mr. Charlie, "Now it's your first day and we are going to start off with a list of our rules. Please abide by them at all times. My right-hand employee Liam will see to it that you are shown around the kitchen and told what to do."

Just as Floza was about to ask Mr. Charlie who Liam was, the kitchen door opened and out stepped a boy. Liam was the right-hand manager for Mr. Charlie. He was rather young, however older than Floza. In fact, he had just finished school and started working at the restaurant. He was very thin and tall with wavy hair which this is why he always had his hair tied up in the kitchen. Liam managed the kitchen including the cooks and dishwashers, so he was behind the scenes at Mr. Charlie's restaurant. Mr. Charlie managed the dining area; he was very good at making sure the customers get what they ordered and the food was up to standard. Mr. Charlie mentioned to Liam that this was the girl starting as the new dishwasher and her name was Floza.

"Pleased to meet you," said Floza, and she extended her hand so as to greet him. Liam was very polite. He extended his hand to greet her back and they both smiled. Little did they know that this was the beginning of a true and strong friendship.

"Mr. Charlie, I think Floza will work best in the washing area. Floza do you know how to wash dishes?" asked Liam.

"Yes, Mr. Liam. I have helped my father all the time doing chores of all sorts. I certainly will be able to do this task," replied Floza.

"Please call me Liam, come through to the kitchen and I will show you around," said Liam. "Mr. Charlie, is there anything else you would like to say to Floza before she starts working?"

"No Liam," replied Mr. Charlie. "Just make sure she gets out of those posh clothes she's wearing. Give her an apron and please girl tie your hair back, washing dishes is not a glam show." Mr. Charlie was very blunt at times but Floza expected this as her friends had warned her of his nature.

"I will do Sir," replied Floza.

"Now come through," said Liam. "We have work to do."

"This.... is the kitchen," said Liam. "These are our two cooks.... Mrs. Long berry and Mrs. Finns."

"Pleased to meet you both," said Floza.

"How old are you girl? You look rather young," asked Mrs. Finns.

Liam looked at Mrs. Finns as to ensure her wandering mind was stopped immediately.

"She... is here to help us with the dishes," said Liam, "And she will answer to no one but me!"

"Certainly Mr. Liam, it's a pleasure to meet you Floza," said Mrs. Longberry.

Mrs. Longberry possessed a quiet nature, she was a very gifted cook. She could make anything from pastries to soups and her food was absolutely delicious.

"She's our star cook, and Mrs. Finn is her apprentice cook," said Liam.

Mrs. Finn had a rather quirky smile and liked to be the center of attention. You can imagine how her face looked. It was green with envy when Liam addressed Mrs. Longberry as being the star cook.

"Now ladies let me leave you to your work," said Liam.

The kitchen was very tidy and everything in its place, further in the back was the washing area.

"This is where you will work." said Liam. "The soap is inside this cupboard and the sponges and clots are in this draw. You will find that the hot water tap is a bit troublesome at times; we are expecting the plumbers in today to sort this out. Greasy dishes need hot water I am sure of that. Do you have any questions Floza?"

"No.... I understand perfectly well my duties, Mr. Liam. Please can I have the apron and cloth to tie my hair. I see there are many dishes waiting to be cleaned," said Floza.

"It's Liam and yes I will get them to you right away. There you go," said Liam.

"Thank you," said Floza and she tied her hair back to begin working.

The day was long and the dishes piled up, there were so many customers in one day. Breakfast and lunch at the restaurant attracted a good crowd – but dinner was the largest, so the staff worked really hard in the evening to ensure the customers were satisfied with their food. Floza's shift finished in the evening and she was exhausted after her first days of work.

"I wish that I was already in bed," thought Floza. She could barely keep her eyes opened but she was also hungry and she was sure Stacy was waiting for her at the dining hall to hear all about her first day.

At the dining hall the lady cats were playing games of chess; they had small teams who competed against each other. They kept busy whilst they were waiting for their meals. Stacy spotted Floza and she made a space available for her so that she could also participate in the game.

"Oh...no. Stacy I am not familiar with this type of game," said Floza. "We usually play outside at Clobet Valley and its quite fun especially during the summer time."

Suddenly the bell rang and the cooks appeared in the Hall way with trays of food that smelt revolting. It was one of the lady cat's birthdays, so the cook had prepared a feast of delectable food. Well delectable according to the cat ladies. Floza usually ordered something different from the menu as she did not trust what the cooks prepared for the Cat people.

"I will have a baked potato thank you Mrs. Cook" said Floza.

"Will that be all for you Miss Floza?" asked the cook.

"Actually, I would not mind having some vegetables on the side, maybe carrots if possible?" replied Floza.

"A baked potato again?" asked Stacy. "That sounds so un-pleasant. Try some of this; it's great."

Stacy offered Floza what looked like liver pate. Floza had to hold her breath when Stacy placed the spoon close to her nose because it smelt so bad.

"Very well then," said Stacy, "Cook. Please bring Flo her vegetables? So, tell me about your day Floza?"

"It was not as bad as you predicted; the work is tedious but the people are okay. I work under a boy named Liam and I personally think he is very nice."

"Well that's good to hear Floza," said Stacy. "For some reason I have been suffering with an itch on my back the entire day. I could not wait to get back to my cat form so I could use my claws to scratch the mites away."

"You have mites?" asked Floza.

"Yes Floza. I am half animal after all, we are bound to get mites or little insects that live in our fur," said Stacy.

"You should shampoo regularly," said Floza.

"Well, I... do!" replied Stacy. "I use one of the 'best' shampoos made by Hendo Enterprises themselves. "Enough about me Floza, tell me more about your day at 'Eat your Heart Out'."

"Well Stacy, it was pretty average," replied Floza, "I did my work well for the first day, at least that is what Liam said."

"Liam? Who's Liam?" asked Stacy.

"Liam is my manager at the restaurant; he manages the kitchen for Mr. Charlie," answered Floza.

"You seem to be very fond off this guy Liam?" asked Stacy.

"I would not say fond. I just feel he is a good person," replied Floza, "And there are not many good people I have met before."

"I hope that I am on your list of good people," said Stacy.

"Of course, you are. I am very fond of our friendship Stacy." Stacy lit up when Floza expressed her fondness for their friendship because she felt the same way.

"I hope you have not forgotten about your audition tonight for the talent show," said Stacy.

"Audition? I'm just kidding. I mean you were going to show me your ballet dancing this evening. I have already arranged with Gracy for the radio," said Stacy.

"What is a radio?" asked Floza.

"Are you joking?" asked Stacy. "This is one of the most important inventions of time – it's music from a box. I love electro beat music in fact most people do at Durbey. I am sure you have noticed the outstanding colors and style of the people of Durbey."

"Yes, I have noticed it is quite different," replied Floza. "Well Stacy, the thing is that I can dance but only to the piano, we usually have live music playing at our ballet practice. Actually, just a person plays the piano and sometimes she sings as well."

"I can assure you it's going to be so much easier using the radio. Are you done with your dinner?" asked Stacy. "Yes, I am Stacy," replied Floza. "Well then, let's get ready for your audition," said Stacy.

"That's fine," said Floza, "I hope you have kept this to yourself Stacy."

It was nine o'clock at night and both Stacy and Floza were in the dining hall. Stacy had put on the music from the radio, a few songs she had recorded some time back. It was electro beat music the sort of music that was very fast and modern.

"I surely cannot dance ballet to this music," said Floza.

"Well I did not expect you to," said Stacy. "I was thinking we mix some piano beats with this music and we see how it goes. Now show me your moves Floza!"

"My moves?" questions Floza.

"Yes, show me how you dance," said Stacy.

Floza began dancing. She tips toed and she finished off with a twirl; her posture was excellent and she had an energy in her that was unexplainable.

"Well done," said Stacy, and she stood up clapping with excitement, "You are quite the dancer, I knew you had it in you."

"I wouldn't say good," said Floza. "I would think my dancing is quite average."

"Don't be silly, you give yourself no credit at all, I am not just saying that because you are my friend," replied Stacy.

"I have not been given any compliments on my dancing before, but maybe it's because I don't dance often," said Floza.

"Floza, I know that you will be great at the talent show," said Stacy.

"Actually, I am not sure I want to take part in the Durbey talent show," said Floza.

"The thing is … I work late hours at 'Eat Your Heart Out'. I really do not have the time to practice."

"I am sure we will find the time to rehearse Floza," said Stacy.

"No Stacy. I don't have time for these things. I came to Durbey for one main reason and taking part in a talent show is irrelevant."

"I am sorry to disappoint you but I have to go to bed now. I have a busy day tomorrow."

Floza stormed out the hall, her hair was falling loose from her plait. Suddenly she felt overwhelmed with the many responsibilities she had to cope with. It was difficult for a young girl living in a strange city.

Stacy was surprised by Floza's reaction, but took no offence, to Floza not wanting to participate in the Durbey Talent Show. There was a reason Stacy wanted Floza to win the Durbey Talent Show, there was something more she knew about, could there be a perk of some kind?

CHAPTER 7

THE STRANGE MAN

At Clobet Valley, Loops was at the town market buying food and household items. He could not help but notice a man standing at the well, which was situated in the middle of the town; he looked very mysterious with his long coat and hat, which covered most of his face. What was strange about this man is that he was very well dressed but seemed to be begging from the people who walked by. This man was definitely someone Loops had never seen before, and it was quite unusual for beggars to be in Clobet Town or any part of the Valley for that matter.

"I need some fruits, and I think Rods would do good with some meaty treats," said Loops.

"Can I have a bunch of grapes?" asked Loops.

"Yes Sir, these are freshly picked," replied the merchant.

"Thank you, I will sure enjoy them..." said Loops "Sir, Sir..." Loops heard someone call him from behind.

"Please help me with something to eat?" It was the strange man...

"I am new to this place, I do not have a place to live nor a thing to eat. I can help you with something," said Loops, and he took a loaf of bread from his basket and placed it in the man's hands.

"Thank you, kind Sir," said the man, "You will surely be blessed," and he walked away to get the attention of others walking past.

"Something is very familiar about that man's voice, but something even more worries me is that he said his not from these parts," thought Loops.

"People have never entered Clobet Valley without our permission, the borders are quite secure. Could it be that the guards at the boarders are failing in their duties?" Loops walked back home to surprise Rods with some meaty treats.

Headmaster Nimble had worked extra hours at the school; since it was a Saturday, he used this time to round up his work. He was all alone at Lilly Ann, he usually worked the weekends, since he did not have a family of his own, and he was usually occupied with work.

"This answer is correct, so is this one..." said Mr. Nimble. "I wonder who this student might be." He turned over the test paper to find out who the excellent student was.

"Suzy Hoppins..." said Headmaster Nimble. "I should have guessed it was Suzy she is always such an excellent student, she takes after her grandfather...."

Headmaster Nimble spent that afternoon marking test papers, when suddenly he heard a noise in the hall way... Dsh-hhhhhhh! It sounded like something had fallen.

"What is that noise?" said Headmaster Nimble. "It seems to come from the hallway. I hope it's not one of those rowdy monkeys again; they always seem to find their way inside the school, wreaking havoc as usual."

So the Headmaster woke up from his seat, to check what all the commotion was about. He stood outside his office, and peeked down the hall way, but there was no one there.

"Strange..." "There seems to be no one here..." So he walked back to his desk to continue with his marking, un-til... he had heard a noise again.

Dshhhhh! It sounded like someone threw an object on the student's lockers.

"That noise again..." So he woke up from his seat once again and walked to the hallway. This time he decided to walk towards the student lockers. As he walked, he noticed a strange man standing next to the water fountain. It was the strange man from the market place, he had made his way to Lilly Ann, but for what reason? "Excuse me," said the Head-master. "What are you doing here?"

"The man replied in a soft voice.... I am looking for the doctor's surgery?"

"I thought this was the place, until I saw the sign Lilly Ann..."

"Oh.... you are certainly in the wrong place, this is a school, as you would have noticed the sign outside. It clear-ly states so," said the Headmaster.

"How stupid of me..." replied the strange man as he hesi-tated upon the Headmasters response.

"I will leave at once, I apologize once again," and he walked briskly away from the school.

"That man was very strange..." thought Headmaster Nimble. "I have not seen him at Clobet Valley before. I will need to ask Loops if he knows about this man entering the Valley."

Clobet Valley was a secret little place, known by the people of Clobet and a few of their distant relatives, who were permitted to visit from time to time. Before these distant relatives visited Clobet Valley, they were required to send through a letter of invitation to the elders mainly Mrs. Poppsy and Loops. It was them who would decide if it was safe to allow the family members to visit.

It was midday, Mrs. Poppsy was working in her garden, grooming her trees and making sure her cherry blossoms were getting enough water. She usually used them as decorations for the Clobet Fair, it was a tradition that had carried on for years, of course introduced by Mrs. Poppsy herself.

It was a scorching day at Clobet, but despite the weather Mrs. Poppsy was still prepared to work in her garden. She wore a big hat while she gardened; it covered most of her face, not forgetting her garden mittens, she had specially sewn.

"Hello my pretties, you are looking marvelous," said Mrs. Poppsy.

She often talked to her plants as if they were human beings. It was her way of keeping busy. Now that Popsicle had disappeared, she felt even more lonely.

"I'll promise to water you every day, you will be just perfect for the Clobet Fair. Everyone will be admiring you... as you are always the star decoration."

"Excuse me old lady..." said a voice. Mrs. Poppsy turned around to see who was there. It was none other than the strange man, he had made his way to Mrs. Poppsy.

"Yes, how can I help you?" replied Mrs. Poppsy. She had never seen the man at Clobet before, he looked mysterious, and the tone of his voice was low.

"I am in search of the town's doctor...You see, I am not feeling well, can you direct me to him?" asked the man.

"Yes certainly, you would need to take this path till the road ends, as you turn to your right, you will find a cottage, it is shaped very much like a turnip. There is also a sign outside that says surgery. It is there that you will find Dr. Hoppins, I can't promise he will be at home though," said Mrs. Poppsy.

"Thanks lady," replied the strange man. He then walked away in the direction mentioned by Mrs. Poppsy.

"I have never seen him around Clobet... this is strange," thought Mrs. Poppsy.

"We would have been alarmed if a foreign person enters the Valley, at least from our guards protecting the border."

After visiting Mrs. Poppsy at her cottage, the strange man walked to Dr. Hoppins home. It was not a far distance to get to the destination. Dr. Hoppins was busy attending to patients, he did get assistance at times from his granddaughter Suzy. She assisted her grandfather to book in patients, and also with some of the administration. The strange man approached Dr. Hoppins cottage, it was indeed shaped like a turnip just as Mrs. Poppsy had described.

"I see the doctor is at home today, just my luck," said the strange man.

He walked to the entrance of the cottage, and found Suzy at the desk with a few patients.

"Hello Sir...are you here to see the doctor?" asked Suzy.

"Yes I am child, does he perhaps have an appointment available?" asked the man.

"Well he is rather busy today.... as you can see." There was a number of patients waiting to be treated. Since Dr. Hoppins was one of few doctors in Clobet, he was always busy.

"Shall I make an appointment for tomorrow?" asked the strange man.

"Let me see what times we have available," replied Suzy.

"I have a morning appointment available, at ten o clock."

"Yes, that will be fine, put my details down for that slot," replied the strange man.

"Your name is?" asked Suzy.

"Well its Mr. Wallens," replied the strange man.

"Can you spell that for me please?" said Suzy.

"W-a-l-l-e-n-s, Mr. Wallens," replied the strange man.

"Thank you Mr. Wallens, I have noted your appointment down for tomorrow. See you then!" smiled Suzy.

"Actually little girl, it seems my shoe is broken, I still have a long way to travel, do you perhaps know of any town cobblers that can help me to fix this wretched shoe?" asked the strange man.

"Why…. yes," you may visit Mr. Thimble.

"He will certainly help to repair that shoe of yours.

Mr. Thimble is the best cobbler in Clobet Valley."

"How fascinating, I would love to pay this Mr. Thimble a visit," replied the strange man.

"Can you direct me to his workshop?"

"Yes, you would need to walk towards the town, at the town you will find Mr. Thimbles workshop, it is not very far from the well," replied Suzy.

"Yes, I know were the well is. Thank you for your information."

The man bid farewell to Suzy, and he marched down the hill towards Clobet town. He did not have a long way to go until he reached the town. It was filled with people, merchants and traders. The strange man approached the well at the center of the town, and to his left he noticed a sign saying shoe repairs. He walked closer to the sign and noticed a little room behind it, it was Mr. Thimbles workshop. It was a small workshop, but it attracted a lot of customers. Inside the workshop was Mr. Thimble, working away on his many orders. The strange man knocked on the door, as to get Mr. Thimbles attention.

"Hello, Sir…. are you the town cobbler?"

"The sign outside says so," replied Mr. Thimble. "What can I do for you?"

"I have a broken shoe, it needs to be fixed, can you help me to repair it?" asked the strange man.

"I am sure I can. Can I have a look at it first, to access the damage?" asked Mr. Thimble.

"Sure….," the man took off his shoe, and handed it to Mr. Thimble.

"Why… this is a very fancy shoe Sir, I am not sure – I will have the materials, to repair this shoe. May I ask, where did you buy these pair of fancy shoes?"

"I got them from the City, in fact they were custom made just for me," replied the strange man.

"The City? Which City?" asked Mr. Thimble.

"It's a City far away… called Urbandew," replied the strange man.

"Urbandew…. I have not heard of that place before," replied Mr. Thimble.

"Are you perhaps visiting family here at Clobet?" "Yes, that's correct…" replied the strange man. "Which family is this?" asked Mr. Thimble.

"The Pollens Family, my distant relatives."

"I see, well since I cannot repair this shoe, you had best be on your way," said Mr. Thimble who felt rather uncomfortable with the man's responses.

"Indeed," replied the strange man. He exited the workshop, quite annoyed his shoe could not be repaired. "That man is not from these parts…. The Pollens family…. we do not have such a family here at Clobet. Who was he trying to fool…besides we would have received an invitation from him to enter our Valley. I need to arrange for a meeting with Mrs. Poppsy and the other elders to see whether they know if this strange man, was invited to come to Clobet."

So Mr. Thimble called the other elders at once. He was panicking after seeing this strange man, he had left him with an unsettling feeling since he could not comprehend who this man really was.

Mr. Thimble had never heard of the Pollens family at Clobet, he was even more concerned about this strange man, and his reason for visiting Clobet Valley.

So he called for the other elders to clarify his doubts... Mrs. Poppsy gather the other elders for a meeting at the town hall. "This is urgent," said Mr. Thimble.

"What is going on Thimble? You sound frightened" asked Mrs. Poppsy.

"I don't have time to explain right now Mrs. Poppsy, but I promise I will when we meet at the Hall," said Mr. Thimble.

It was six in the evening and the meeting between the elders of Clobet Valley had started. Mr. Thimble started the meeting, since he had called the other elders.

"Dear friends. Something really strange.... happened today, whilst I was working. I met a man, he wore a long coat and a hat that covered most of his face. This man was rather strange, he approached me at my workshop, something about wanting his broken shoe fixed. It was a fine pair of shoes, I say, not even I can craft such to perfection. Since I could not repair his shoe, I sent him off, but what worries me about this man... is not because I could not repair his shoe, no.... further to our conversation, I asked him if he was a visitor to this place, and he said he was here to visit distant relatives, namely the Pollens family."

"Pollens family?" asked Loops. "But we don't have such a family with that name."

"Well if he's not from here how did he get here?" asked Dr. Hoppins.

"That is the very reason I have called this meeting, for us to find out who this man is and – what business he has at Clobet."

"Actually, I noticed this man today," said Mrs. Poppsy, "Whilst I was gardening he approached me, he wore a long coat and a hat which covered his face, just as you have described."

"You have encountered the same man?" asked Mr. Thimble.

"It seems so," replied Mrs. Poppsy.

"Actually, I have seen a man in the market place today, he was begging, and yes, he resembled the very same man you speak of," replied Loops.

"What about you Nimble, did you not notice this man?" asked Loops.

"Yes, I did," replied Headmaster Nimble. "You see I was completing some off my marking today at Lilly Ann, when I heard a strange noise. I decided to find out what this noise was, until I found a man standing in the hall way. It was the same man you speak of. I asked him what business he had coming to the school. He said that it was a mistake, he was actually looking for the doctor's surgery.... I felt this was very strange since the sign outside clearly states 'Lilly Ann'."

"My point exactly," said Mr. Thimble. "This man had lied, he obviously was uninvited, unless any off you have received an invitation recently?"

"I have not received any outside invitations," replied Mrs. Poppsy.

"Nor did I," replied Loops.

Mrs. Poppsy and Loops were specifically nominated to deal with all outside invitations sent through to Clobet Valley. Both Loops and Mrs. Poppsy were well aware of the families who lived at Clobet Valley, in fact there were not many.

The visitors rule was that immediate family members were allowed to come to Clobet Valley, in this way not many people knew about Clobet Valley. The elders of the Valley made sure that there were strict controls placed, to ensure no wandering persons would enter the Valley. You are probably thinking why place such strict controls, after all it was a small Valley. We will find out later as to why the elders of Clobet Valley protected their perfect little world. Dr. Hoppins was the only elder that had not met this strange man.

"I did not come across this strange man," said Dr. Hoppins.

"Interesting as to why he would skip me?"

"I don't think he skipped you," replied Mrs. Poppsy. "I did see him briskly walking in the direction to your cottage."

"He had specifically asked to see you – since he was feeling unwell."

"Strange… thought Dr. Hoppins, I do not recall seeing any patient resembling this strange man. Perhaps I missed him? I shall ask my granddaughter Suzy, she was assisting me on the day, recording my appointments, perhaps she came across him."

"Great idea," said Headmaster Nimble. "Surely she would have seen this strange man at your surgery."

"I think its best we gather more information about this strange man. Hoppins, you try and find more information about this man from Suzy…" said Loops.

"Thimble and I will approach the guards at the borders, I think the best way forward is to ask the guards if they perhaps had seen a person trying to get in the valley? Mrs. Poppsy, you try and do a sketch of this strange man, with a combination of all our descriptions. This will help us to get a visual of who we are dealing with. We will meet the day after tomorrow, to present our evidence. Please keep this amongst us for now, until…. we find more facts about – this strange man."

So the elders agreed to follow Loops instruction's before they parted ways.

CHAPTER 8

THE SURPRISE

Meanwhile at 'Eat your heart out', Liam and Floza were preparing for a big dinner. It was a wealthy business owner's wife's birthday, and many of the rich and elite people in Durbey were attending. Mr. Charlie ordered his staff to use all the finest dinner plates and accessories. All the staff received special instructions to look their finest. Mr. Charlie stood at the entrance of the restaurant dressed in his suit, to welcome his quests.

"Mrs. Groans, welcome to 'Eat Your Heart Out'," said Mr. Charlie.

"We have prepared our special menu just for your birthday."

Mrs. Groans was a fashionable lady, who always wore a hat on her head. She was the wife of Mr. Groans who was in the electronic appliance business. Tonight was very special since it was her birthday, tonight her hat looked rather unique. It had a feather on it, it was glamorous.

"I have extra staff working on your meals, Mrs. Groans. Liam here will see to it that your meals arrive on time," said Mr. Charlie.

"Yes Mam," said Liam, in a confident manner.

"I must say you look ravishing and not a day over fifty," said Mr. Charlie.

"At what time will Mr. Groans be joining you?"

"Mr. Charlie, you are too kind," replied Mrs. Groans as she blushed.

"I am looking forward to dinner this evening, Mr. Groans will be here at any moment. He had an urgent business matter to attend to. I have heard you prepare the most delectable roast duck," said Mrs. Groans.

"Indeed, and we have added it to your birthday menu.
Let me show you to your seat," said Mr. Charlie.

"Roast Duck! How could she want that?" thought Floza.

Floza thought about the animals at Clobet Valley, like the time she freed most of Dr. Hoppins animals from his yard. She had a soft spot for animals, especially birds. Tonight she felt rather revolted that Mrs. Groans had chosen duck on her menu.

"You look rather upset," said Liam.

"No, I am perfectly fine," replied Floza.

"Then why are you squeezing that lemon so tightly and your face is looking rather red, Floza," asked Liam.

"I don't know what you mean," replied Floza. "Never mind," said Liam.

"We have a busy night, please make sure all the dishes are crystal clear. We have to make an impression tonight. Our service tonight will determine our customers for the future. Imagine if so many rich customers visited our restaurant all the time, Mr. Charlie will be a wealthy man, and maybe he will be a less stressed man," giggled Liam.

"I heard my name, Liam," said Mr. Charlie.

"Oh no Sir, I was just explaining to cooks, the cranberry sauce needs to be runnier," replied Liam.

"Please stop chattering and see to our guests," shouted Mr. Charlie.

"Right away Sir," replied Liam.

The restaurant ended up with so many guests that evening. There was laughter and conversation amongst the guests. The very elite were the guests of Mr. Charlie, they mostly socialized together, since they had one thing in common, they were rich beyond measure.

These business owners were powerful, yes, but there was one person even more powerful in the whole of Durbey, Mr. Hendo Wallens. In fact, most of these businesses relied on Hendo Enterprises for their operations. It was Mr. Hendo who encouraged a few people in Durbey to open their own businesses, but it was still governed by him. In fact, nothing in Durbey was independent, everything was owned or controlled by Mr. Hendo.

The phone rang.

"Hello, yes this is Liam speaking. How may I help you?" asked Liam.

"This is nurse Hatty calling from the Durbey Hospital," said a voice. "I am calling regarding your father Mr. Luke."

"Nurse Hatty?" asked Liam. "What about my father? Is he okay?" "Please tell me nurse?"

"He is okay for now," replied the nurse.

"What do you mean?" said Liam.

"Well, while your father was busy working, he had a heart attack and so he was rushed to Durbey Hospital," said the nurse.

"Heart Attack!!, my father, I'll come right away!! Mr. Charlie, Mr. Charlie!!" yelled Liam.

"What is it boy? You looked flustered."

"Well Mr. Charlie, I have just heard that my father has had a heart attack. He is now at Durbey hospital, not in a very good condition. I will have to go and see him urgently," said Liam.

"What!" said Mr. Charlie, "You can't leave now! We have important guests."

"It's okay Mr. Charlie. I can assist with Liam's duties while he is away," said Floza.

"Yes," said Mrs. Finns and Longberry, "We will assist Floza while Liam's away."

"Floza, are you sure you want to help?" asked Liam.

"Yes," said Floza. "Family is the most important thing in our lives. I will see to it that your chores are done," replied Floza.

"Wait a minute, I did not give you permission to leave this restaurant," said Mr. Charlie.

"But this is an emergency," replied Liam. "I promise I will be back as fast as I can."

"No is no..." said Mr. Charlie. "You are not allowed to leave."

"I would have thought you of all people would not understand the importance of family," said Liam.

"After all, you gave up your own wife, just for your opportunity to own this restaurant; it was all for power and money!"

There was silence in the kitchen, all the staff were shocked at what Liam had just said. In fact, everyone knew that Mr.

Charlie had left his wife, just so he could save his restaurant. Mr. Charlie needed a loan from the Hendo bank, but he was married to an employee of Hendo Enterprises and this was not possible.

He had decided to leave his wife to pursue his dream of owning a successful restaurant "Keep quiet boy!!" yelled Mr. Charlie. "You know nothing of my family affairs!"

"I do, Mr. Charlie. Who here does not know?" He looked around the kitchen as if to get approval from the other workers. It seemed, by the expressions on their faces, that they clearly knew of what Liam spoke off.

"Why you have got a nerve," said Mr. Charlie. "You think you are irreplaceable boy. As of now you are not allowed to come back here, you are officially fired!!"

"What?" said Liam. "After everything I have done for you Mr. Charlie? I saved you from bankruptcy, you were to be destroyed," shouted Liam.

"No boy, I saved myself," said Mr. Charlie. "In fact, the only person I owe gratitude to is Mr. Hendo; if it were not for his loan, this place would not be running. Now leave immediately!!"

"No, this can't be happening," said Floza. "Don't leave Liam, Mr. Charlie is just under pressure."

"No Floza, Mr. Charlie knows very well what I speak of." said Liam.

"My father needs me, I have to go."

Liam stormed out of the kitchen, flung his apron aside and walked off to attend to his father, Mr. Luke. "Don't come back!" yelled Mr. Charlie.

"I can't believe what just happened," thought Floza. "I feel Mr. Charlie is being unreasonable. What was it that Liam said about Mr. Charlie giving up his wife for money? Could it be Stacy was right all along? After all she warned me about Mr. Charlie. I did not listen to her, but I needed a job so desperately to pay for my hostel fee. I don't blame Liam. Why… if father was ill, I would do the same. I hope Mr. Luke is okay; I have not met him before, but I have heard he is a really nice man."

"Floza!! You will see to the guests this evening," said Mr. Charlie. "I can't believe I am doing this but we are short staffed, we can't afford to disappoint Mr. and Mrs. Groans. Mrs. Finns, see to it that she changes her uniform. You can't be looking like that working in front, it's a different game out there."

"I may just have a white coat lying around," said Mrs. Finns. "Here you go girl, you can change into this."

Mrs. Finns threw the coat at Floza. She was under pressure, so many dishes were for tonight's guests. Floza put on the coat, tied her hair back and took a deep breath.

"I can do this!" she said. "All I have to do is ask the guests if their meals are fine." Floza entered the front of the restaurant; the restaurant had never been this full.

"Don't disappoint me," said Mr. Charlie. "Go on and attend to that table."

Floza walked towards the table. At the table was a man, he was in fact the same man who had yelled at her when he had tripped over his walking stick.

"Good evening are the meals fine?" she asked.

"Why don't you ask them yourself?" said the man.

"Ha, Ha, Ha," and everyone at the table began to join him laughing.

"I beg your pardon Sir," asked Floza.

"You look familiar girl. Have we met before?" asked the man.

"No… no… I don't think we have," replied Floza.

"We need another bottle of wine for our table!" ordered the man.

"I'll see to it that you get it right away, Sir," said Floza.

Another guest called, "Waiter! Please get me some more bread."

"Yes, I will get you some, right away." Floza walked briskly to the kitchen and requested the wine and bread. She delivered the request to her guests, only to find that she had mixed up the orders.

"We wanted wine, not bread, how stupid can you be? It was just a simple order," said the guest.

"I am sorry Sir," replied Floza. "She felt rather embarrassed after mixing up the guests orders.

"I have never come across people like this at Clobet Valley," thought Floza. "These people are so mean..."

It was after a long evening, playing dual roles at the restaurant, that Floza returned to Eva's women's hostel. Tonight's experience had opened her eyes to what the outside world was really like. Durbey was a place where people were separated according to what they owned, it was an absolute contrast of the society of Clobet Valley. As Floza walked in the entrance of the hall, the watch on the wall turned to eight o clock.

"It is quite late now," she said. "I doubt Stacy will be awake at this hour." The hostel was very quiet, all the ladies were asleep at this time.

"I'll get ready for bed now," said Floza. She pulled aside the covers and got into bed, then laid her head on her pillow. She was about to doze off, when suddenly she heard a voice

"Wake up Flo!!" It was none other than Stacy.

"I stayed up, waiting for you!" she said.

"But why? Its rather late, and I am rather tired," replied Floza.

"I was so excited I could not sleep," said Stacy. "Why are you so excited Stacy?" asked Floza.

"I found something out today about the Durbey Talent Show," said Stacy.

"You are still going on about that, I thought I made it clear last night that I am not taking part," said Floza.

"Floza, please listen to me, there is a prize to be won. The person that is voted the best and most talented will win a prize," Stacy said excitedly.

"What sort of prize...?" asked Floza.

"It's not just any prize it's one of Mr. Hendo's inventions. This makes it much more of a competition since there is a prize involved," explained Stacy.

"Well I don't really need anything," said Floza. "Unless it's something that will help me get the cure for father much faster," she thought.

"So the invention is none other than ...... a teleporting-bubble!!" said Stacy.

"Teleporting bubble," repeated Floza.

"Yes! Imagine all the fun we could have with that!" Floza's eyes lit up with contentment; her pale face, took on a rosy hue, after Stacy mentioned the grand prize being none other than the teleporting bubble.

"If I could win the talent show I could use the teleporting bubble to travel back to Clobet Valley," she thought.

"Maybe it would help me to travel to other places to get the cure for father much faster."

"Stacy .... I have changed my mind I have decided to take part in the talent show," said Floza.

"See! I knew I could convince you to participate," replied Stacy, excited that Floza had agreed to compete in the talent show.

The girls spent the night talking about how they intended on planning the best act which would win first place at the Durbey Talent show. Floza was now very excited on hearing the good news about the prize to be won. There was no way she would not stand in line to win the teleporting bubble; after all, the bubble could transport her back to Clobet Valley.

"Once I get the cure from Edor, I will use the bubble to go back home," she thought.

"What ever would we use the teleporting bubble for?" she asked Stacy.

"If there is one place I would go… it would be Galley town, my home town," replied Stacy.

"I thought that Durbey was your home town Stacy?" asked Floza, puzzled.

"Actually Floza… I was born in Galley town, my parents then moved to Durbey a few years ago," explained Stacy. She grabbed Floza and spun around with excitement. "We will need to go shopping, you will have to look unique like one of us Durbey citizens. We'll pick you something bright and illuminating for the Durbey Talent show, and when you twirl you will look just like a firework!"

"A firework?" asked Floza.

"Yes, the most beautiful site in Durbey…." smiled Stacy.

CHAPTER 9

THE DURBEY EXPRESS

Floza did not mention to Stacy, or anyone for that matter, the incident between Liam and Mr. Charlie. She thought that after the little commotion, Mr. Charlie would have forgotten about the argument between him and Liam; in a perfect world Mr. Charlie would have realized his mistake and so would Liam, but this was not the case.

Mr. Charlie had no remorse for Liam losing his job, in fact he did not care at all. The very next day Floza woke up very early to start her day. It was her day off from work, since there had been many guests the night before. Mr. Charlie had made a lot of money and closed the restaurant for the entire day.

"What shall I do today?" thought Floza. "Stacy is occupied at work... most of the ladies are not here. Unless... I visit Liam? After the argument yesterday and him losing his job I am sure he will need a friend. It would also be a good idea to visit Mr. Luke since he has not been well. I would need to take a bath first. At least with the ladies gone I can spend more time in the bathroom."

It was always quite a rush in the mornings, especially since the ladies shared a bath room. It was quite big with many showers and tubs, but because there were so many women who left in early hours of the morning, it did become a bit chaotic. Floza entered the bathroom, with her bath brush in one hand and shower cap in the other.

"I do hope they saved me some hot water," said Floza. She ran the water in the bath tub, and it was the perfect temperature. She then left the water to run, to fill the tub. Floza then walked towards the wash area, to look at her reflection in the mirror. She leaned over the wash area, to look at her image.

"I look rather tired," she said. "My hair has grown very long; I shall tie it up today."

As she looked in the mirror, she could not help but notice a door right behind her. It was marked with a no entry sign.

"That is strange," she thought. "I have never seen this door before." Just as she was about to open it, Gracy walked in.

"Stop! What do you think you are doing?" she said. "Can you not see the sign Floza?" asked Grace. "Mmm... good morning Gracy," said Floza. She was amazed that Gracy had walked in at that moment; she felt rather scared. Floza waited for Gracy to react, as she knew what she was about to do was against the hostel rules.

"Answer me Floza? Why were you trying to open that door?" demanded Gracy.

"I am… sorry Gracy, I did not notice the sign and I was looking for the towels. I just got mixed up with the doors, I thought it was a closet," said Floza.

Gracy stared at Floza, she had felt rather upset when she had seen Floza breaking the rules. But Floza was lucky, she had caught Gracy on a good day.

"Oh, I see, you are quite new… it does happen," replied Gracy.

"However, make sure that in future you will be more vigilant of the signs."

"Certainly Gracy, I do apologize… I will definitely be more careful going forward," replied Floza.

"Good! I have to see to the housekeeping now. Later then," said Gracy

"Have a good day," said Floza, to make Gracy feel at ease.

"I am such a clutz," said Floza.

"I could have got into big trouble. I would have been kicked out of the women's hostel for breaking the rules. Phew!" said Floza with a sigh of relief. Something had stuck in Floza's mind that morning; it was the whole incident in the bathroom that she could not quite make sense of. "Firstly…." she thought.

"I have never seen that door before, why would it have no entry? What is behind it? It must be something important, or else Gracy would not have reacted in the way she did. I am sure Stacy will know about it. I'll ask her when she gets back from 'The Cherry on Top'."

Floza dressed up, she then went to the dining hall to have her breakfast.

"I see you are the only one here," said Chef Prudence. "You may order whatever you like from the menu, it's our little secret."

"Thank you, Chef Prudence," said Floza as she smiled. "I do have a long day ahead off me, I would like to order from the lunch menu."

"Sure, here you go, Floza. This is our lunch menu," said the chef.

"Chef Prudence, would you perhaps know where Olive place is situated?" asked Floza.

"Why would you be going to Olive place?" asked Chef Prudence.

"It is very run down, it's nothing like Durbey town, I would say it's more laid back."

"Well…. I have a friend whom I would like to visit. His father is not doing well and I would like to pay them a visit," said Floza sadly.

"Oh dear… that's terrible, I will be glad to help you in any way," said Chef Prudence.

"In fact, you would need to travel there using the Durbey Express Train."

"Durbey Express Train?" asked Floza, "but where would I find this train?"

"You would need to pass Florence Gardens until you come to the Durbey Station; there you will find a booking booth. You will need to buy a ticket, to get on the train and a return for on your way back. Now Floza, I must leave, I have to prepare for tonight's dinner," replied Chef Prudence.

"I would never have found my way if you had not directed me, thank you Chef Prudence." Floza got up from her seat and gave Chef Prudence a hug; she was very happy that she had a friend who could direct her around Durbey.

Later on, she walked along the streets of Durbey, until she came to Florence Gardens.

"I must be close to the station," said Floza. She walked past Florence Gardens. It was looking radiant as ever, filled with cherry blossoms.

"This looks a lot like Mrs. Poppsy's Garden," thought Floza. "I wonder how father is doing, I miss him so much, and Rods. Only a week until I get the cure from Edor, then I am back home at Clobet Valley. In a way, I do enjoy visiting another place, just I wish father and Rods were with me to enjoy this City."

The train tracks were situated slightly differently at Durbey, they were not on the ground, but resembled a roller coaster. The train travelled high up in the City over and between the buildings. It made the city look like a theme park, although it looked quite scary to travel by train. It was actually a very fun experience.

Floza approached the station; it was very busy with many people walking past. Many people at Durbey travelled by train and so the station was always busy. She approached a hallway, and in the hallway sat numerous people behind closed doors. They were workers at the ticket booking booth, and at the entrance of the hall was a screen that displayed travel destinations and times of departure. Olive Place next travel departure is at eleven am, read Floza. I still have time, let me stand in the line to buy my ticket.

"Next customer!!!" called a man from the ticket booth.

It was Floza's turn to buy her ticket.

"Good Morning Miss, what can I do for you?" asked the man, politely.

"Good Morning to you, I am Floza and I need a ticket to travel to Olive Place," answered Floza.

"Sure, we still have seats available for the next trip, that will be two silvers," said the man.

Floza reached into her pocket, only to find that she did not have any money. She had forgotten her purse at home, and at this moment she felt so frustrated about her irresponsible behavior.

"Uhhhh, actually sir, I have changed my mind," she said, and she walked away from the ticket booth.

"How could I be so forgetful!" thought Floza.

"Now what do I do, it will take me a long time to walk to the hostel. In that time I will miss the first departure to Olive Place. Things are not going my way today; first the encounter with Gracy, now this."

Floza was disappointed that her trip to visit Liam and his father was not going according to plan. She walked away feeling rather down. She was about to cross the street to move away from Durbey Station when a car stopped in front of her. It was a posh car. Floza did not know what a car was, to her these machines were foreign to her eyes, since such means of transportation did not exist at Clobet Valley. The car door opened and out stepped a lady, with a fancy hat. She was dropped off by her driver outside Durbey Station; this lady looked quite familiar. Floza had seen her before, but she could not quite remember where. Oh yes! It was the guest from the restaurant Mrs. Groans. She was a very wealthy lady, it was expected she be escorted in a fancy car, with her very own driver.

"Thank you, France," said Mrs. Groans.

"Be sure to pick me up tomorrow at the very same spot."

"Yes…! Mam," replied the driver.

She closed the door and the car drove off. The lady could not help but notice Floza, as she was standing right in front of her.

"Good Morning, little girl," said Mrs. Groans.

"Good Morning too you, Mrs. Groans," said Floza. "Why… how do you know my name girl?"

"I saw you last night at the restaurant, it was your birthday," replied Floza.

"How delightful!" replied Mrs. Groans, "Did you perhaps come with the Simon's family?"

"No… actually, I work for Mr. Charlie, at the restaurant," said Floza. Mrs. Groans was a very down to earth and kind lady. She did not look down on Floza when she mentioned she worked for Mr. Charlie. In fact, Mrs. Groans was one of very few nice wealthy people at Durbey.

"So where are you off too all alone?" asked Mrs. Groans.

"Well... I was on my way to the station to visit my friend Liam; he lives in Olive Place," said Floza.

"But you are walking away from the station, are you not?" asked Mrs. Groans.

"I sort of forgot my purse at home – I will visit him another time," replied Floza.

"Oh, don't be silly," said Mrs. Groans.

"You have already walked all this way I presume. Here, take this money," she said, and she held out her hand with four silvers.

"No Mrs. Groans, I couldn't!" exclaimed Floza.

"Yes you can, take it as a tip for last night's magnificent birthday dinner," replied Mrs. Groans.

Floza hesitated, as she did not want to appear needy. But Mrs. Groans insisted, besides she had not really received any tips for last night's hard work. She took the four silvers from Mrs. Groan's hands and she bowed, lifting her dress and lowering her head.

"Thank you very much, Mrs. Groans," said Floza. "Only a pleasure," said Mrs. Groans.

"I'd best be off.... I am visiting my mother in Port Galley."

"You mean Galley Town?" asked Floza.

"Yes its Galley Town but close to the sea," answered Mrs. Groans.

"Have a safe trip Mrs. Groans," said Floza. They both bid farewell and went their separate ways.

"What a nice lady," thought Floza.

"Now I can get my ticket." So she ran to the ticket booth as fast as she could, before the train departed for Olive Place.

"One ticket to Olive Place," asked Floza.

"You are back," said the man in the ticket booth.

"I changed my mind again," she giggled, excited that her chain of bad events had turned in her favor.

"All aboard the train...." shouted the train master. He looked rather different from your typical train master. He wore a silver jacket, black glasses, and his shoes were very trendy.

"Oh my goodness, I'd better hurry before I miss the train." Floza ran to the train, which was already loaded with passengers.

"Ticket?" asked the train master.

"Here you are Sir," said Floza. He took out a device from his pocket, which scanned the ticket with a blue light.

"Thank you," said the train master, "You may board the train. Your coach is .... C twelve, you will find it next to the candy shop."

"Candy shop?" asked Floza, "In the train?"

"Yes," replied the train master, "There are a number of shops inside the train. Now go in.... and see for yourself, you won't be disappointed."

Floza stood at the entrance of the train. The door opened for her to walk through. When she stepped inside, she was amazed. It looked like a big hotel. It was much bigger than it looked from outside; there were restaurants and shops just like the station master had said.

"Welcome to Durbey Express," said a lady dressed in uniform which looked quite similar to that of the station master.

"You need to take the elevator to coach C," you will find it next to the candy store.

"How is it possible the train looks so big inside? It's more like a building," asked Floza.

"It's one of Mr. Hendo's great inventions," replied the lady.

"He cast a spell off illusion so that the people of Durbey could enjoy this spectacular means of transportation. What you see inside is just an illusion, but it does wonders, look how beautiful it looks inside."

"It does," replied Floza.

"Now how do I go to coach C again?"

"You would need to take the elevator," the lady replied. "What is an elevator?" asked Floza.

"It is a box which you will step inside and it will carry you to your place of destination."

"Are you not from these parts, little girl?" asked the lady.

"No, I am not actually… Thank you Miss, I will go to this elevator and find my way," answered Floza.

"Do enjoy, be sure to try out the candy from the candy store. You will surely enjoy it," said the lady.

"I will," said Floza as she waved goodbye.

Candy…. the last time she had eaten candy was at Clobet Valley. Floza thought about the one-time Mrs. Poppsy had made her homemade bubble gum; it was quite delicious.

"I am sure Mrs. Poppsy is feeling rather lost without Popsicle," thought Floza. "If she only knew that her dear Popsicle was in fact a panther. She would have been terrified. I am sure she would have regretted being so nice to her cat. Now where is that elevator?"

"Excuse me Sir, do you perhaps know where I can find the elevator?" Floza asked a passing man. "Which coach are you going to?" he asked. "Coach C…." replied Floza.

"Then all you need to do is walk down this aisle and take your first left. You will find the elevator, in the corner next to the candy store," said the man.

"Thank you," said Floza. She followed the man's instructions. She walked straight down the aisle, until she took a left turn and she saw the candy store, and there was the elevator.

She had seen the moving box the lady had spoken of. It moved.... straight, and up into the air, transporting people to their coaches. Floza decided to get some candy before she went to her coach.

She walked into the candy store; it was a big store filled with all varieties of treats of all colors and flavors. The candy was brightly-colored and the shop smelt like heaven. She picked some candy to try out and went to the counter to pay for her treats.

"Be careful your candy does not run away," warned the cashier.

"Run away? Whatever do you mean?" said Floza.

The cashier replied, "Well you picked the 'crawling squeegees', they usually don't stick around for too long. Do you think that when you are travelling in a magical train that you would get normal candy?"

"I don't know what is normal anymore," replied Floza, and she left the shop to walk towards the elevator.

She put some of the candy in her mouth; it was delicious.

"I'll keep these for later," she said.

As she got to the elevator, the door opened and she walked inside. There were other people waiting to be transported.

"Which coach are you going to?" asked a man. "I am going to coach C," replied Floza.

"We are all going to Coach C," said the man, and she reached for her ticket inside her pocket.

"My apologies. I am going to coach C twelve," she said.

The man pressed a button, the elevator closed and up it went into the air. It stopped and all the people walked out, pushing each other as if at any time the elevator was about to move.

Just as Floza was about to walk out, the man stopped her. He seemed to be controlling the elevator for the people ensuring they reach their correct coaches.

"Hold on!" said the man, "This is coach eleven, you are still one floor up." 'Coach twelve' lit up inside the elevator. "This is my stop," thought Floza. She walked out to find her seat. The coach was rather big, like a large room, it was occupied with only four people. There were all sorts of interesting things inside, couches, videos on the wall and more treats!

"Would you care for a cup?" asked a young girl.

"A cup of coffee?... and you must try the cake it's to die for...".

A girl just a bit older than Floza was also a passenger on the Durbey Express. She was very friendly and offered Floza her company, over a cup of coffee and cake.

"Sure," replied Floza. "I don't mind having a cup of coffee, and as for the cake, I love cake. Floza noticed the many different varieties of cakes that were displayed, brightly colored and decorated beautifully. They both sat down on the couches while watching the videos on the wall.

"My name is Floza, by the way."

"Oh! I am sorry, how rude of me!" said the girl. "All that excitement about cake and I forgot to introduce myself! I am Alice.... so where are you travelling to Floza?"

"I am going to Olive Place to visit a friend of mine," replied Floza.

"Olive Place, really?" asked the girl. "Yes," said Floza, "Why do you ask?"

"Well I am travelling there myself. I am going to visit my grandmother, I visit every month. She lives all alone and well, I also get lonely at times. We are quite close my Grammy and I," said Alice.

"That sounds lovely...." said Floza. "These cakes are delicious, and the detail is to perfection. Could it be that these are from Mr. Steven's Bakery?" asked Floza. "My friend Stacy works there, and she showed me pictures of the work she has done, the most delectable cakes are made at that bakery."

"Mr. Stevens…, are you sure? That your friend works for Mr. Stevens bakery?" asked Alice.

"Yes, I am, very sure. She goes to work for him every day, he's such a perfectionist Mr. Stevens," said Floza.

"Yes he is….," said Alice. "I know very well about Mr. Stevens. My mother used to work for him."

"Used to, I am sorry is your mother no more?" asked Floza.

"No actually, Mr. Stevens is no more," replied Alice. "He passed on many years ago. He was a very well-known baker in Durbey, and there are not many bakers here, so we must be speaking of the same Stevens."

"'The Cherry on Top?" asked Floza.

"Yes, 'The Cherry on Top', that is where my mother used to work," confirmed Alice.

"But it can't be," thought Floza, "Where is Stacy going every day if she is not working at the 'Cherry on Top'?"

"Attention Passengers! The Durbey Express is ready to take off, please fasten your seat belts."

"It's time for takeoff!" said Alice. "Fasten your seat belt…"

Both the girls fastened their seat belts and the train took off at an exhilarating speed. The Durbey Express made many stops on the way, between and over buildings. The people were transported directly to their offices and homes.

"Care for some candy Alice?" asked Floza as she reached into her pocket.

"Yes please, I cannot say no too candy either…" replied Alice.

Floza shuffled around in her pocket to find the candy; it was in a bag. She took out the bag and opened it, offering Alice the candy. Alice reached inside for the candy, but there was nothing inside…

"But this bag is empty," said Alice.

"It can't be," replied Floza. "I just bought these candies a few minutes ago. The lady at the Candy store called them 'crawling squeegees'.""

"Well no wonder they are not there anymore, those candies don't stay put for too long. You have to eat them immediately," said Alice.

"So the lady at the Candy Store was not kidding when she said be careful, they don't run away?" questioned Floza.

"Yes," replied Alice. "Did you not notice them crawling away from your pocket?"

"No actually, I was trying to find my way around the Durbey Express, I did not notice," said Floza.

"Next Stop Olive Place!" said the voice from the train… "That's our stop," said Floza.

"Yes, it is," replied Alice.

The girls got up and walked out of the coach or should I say 'fancy room with interesting things'.

"How do we get off here?" asked Floza.

"We have to walk to the exit which is downstairs, so we have to take the elevator again," said Alice. So the girls travelled down to the exit, as they reached their destination. They came to a place that was very green, with lots of olive trees. No wonder it was called Olive Place.

"Do you know where about in Olive Place you are going?" asked Alice.

"Yes, my friend Liam, he lives near the Olive Farm, he lives there with his father Luke. He has not been well lately," said Floza.

"Olive Farm, why that is where my Grammy lives, we both shall walk there together," said Alice. The girls walked through the meadows of olive trees. It was a serene place which reminded Floza of Clobet Valley.

"I had no idea that Durbey had places that were as laid back as this," said Floza.

"There are quite a few quite places in Durbey, but no place is like Durbey City," replied Alice.

"You are right about that, Alice!" agreed Floza.

The houses at Olive Place were tiny, it looked like they were getting lost in the trees. Alice caught sight off her grandmother's home as she walked with Floza. It was a tiny house, white in color with a fence around it. In the garden stood an old lady, she wore a brightly colored shawl and it seemed as if she was doing some chores. "That's my grandma's home right ahead of us," said Alice. "Oh and look! Grammy is outside gardening. I would sure like for you to meet her. Grammy, Grammy," called Alice as she waved.

"Well, aren't I glad to see you," said Grammy. "Alice, my good granddaughter."

"Hello Grammy," said Alice as she extended her arms to hug her.

"And who is your new friend?" asked Grammy. "Grammy, this is Floza. We met on the Durbey Express," said Alice.

"That's delightful! Pleased to meet you Floza. What are you doing in Olive Place? Not that I mind, we do enjoy company!" said Grammy.

"Pleased to meet you too Grammy," replied Floza. "I am in fact here to visit my friend Liam and his father Mr. Luke"

"Is that so?" asked Grammy.

"Yes Grammy," replied Floza.

"Why, Mr. Luke has not been well, has he? They live just next to me in that little house," said Grammy. It seemed that Liam was actually Grammy's neighbor.

"Would you like to have some tea, Floza?" asked Grammy.

"It must have been a long journey to Olive Place, you girls must be starving. I have made some steam bread and stew, just how you like it Alice."

"That's the reason I always enjoy coming to Grammy's house, she always spoils me," said Alice.

"Floza, do stay for lunch?" asked Alice.

"Oh no I could not. I have to get going and leave before the sun sets," replied Floza. "Although Grammy's food does sound so delicious. I am sure it tastes delicious too. Steamed bread... I have not eaten that since father prepared his pea soup." She thought of her father and all the delicious meals he had tried to prepare for her.

"I have prepared enough for us all, do come in," said Grammy.

"Okay," said Floza, "I will join you for lunch." They all went inside Grammys cottage, it was filled with knitted accessories and smelt so delicious. Grammy laid the table, and they sat down to eat. It was then time for Floza to leave. She thanked Alice and Grammy. "Do visit again," said Alice. She now went off to visit Liam and his father.

Floza stood outside Liam's house. It was very quiet, and it looked like no one was at home. She stepped up to the door and knocked; the floor creaked with every step she took. It was a little rundown, the house, and now that Liam had lost his job things would be even more difficult.

"Wait a moment," shouted Liam. He was at home. He opened the door and to his surprise he found Floza standing outside.

"Floza! How did you get here? It is so good to see you... I am sorry I stormed off the other night. I had to see to my father. He was not well, in fact he's still in the same condition," said Liam.

"Well, I took the Durbey Express. I hope I am not intruding," said Floza, "But I wanted to see how you were doing and I was worried about your father as well." "That is so thoughtful off you," said Liam. "Now do come inside."

Floza stepped into the cottage, and the floors creaked once again. There were just basics inside the house; it was neat and tidy, even though it did not have fancy things.

"Luckily I just put the kettle on. Would you care for some tea?" asked Liam.

"I was just preparing some for father."

"No, I actually just had some lunch, but thank you Liam." replied Floza.

"Father will be so glad he has a visitor," said Liam. "Let us go to his room, he has been in bed all day, since the incident." Liam walked to his father's room, with a cup of tea in his hands, and Floza followed. She had never met Mr. Luke before, she felt a bit nervous, on seeing him for the first time. "Father, we have a visitor all the way from Durbey Town."

"Come in Floza," said Liam. Floza walked into the room, and in the bed lay Mr. Luke. He was looking very unwell. He tried to smile when he saw Floza, he was glad she had come to visit him.

"Hello Floza," said Mr. Luke in a soft voice, "Come closer to the bed. I have heard so much about you from Liam, thank you for being a friend too him," said Mr. Luke.

"Mr. Luke, I have heard that you were very unwell, I was also concerned that Liam had left his job," replied Floza.

"Yes, Liam told me all about what happened, difficult man that Mr. Charlie," said Mr. Luke.

"Work is work," said Liam, "I'll get another one, even though jobs are hard to come by in Durbey."

"I was thinking Liam, maybe you should speak to Mr. Charlie, to get your job back?" asked Floza. "It is a just a suggestion, I have seen how you've worked at the restaurant, you are really good at what you do."

"There is no chance of that happening," said Liam. "I appreciate your suggestion but I honestly don't see myself working for Mr. Charlie anymore."

"I.... understand," said Floza. "Your father, he works for Hendo Enterprises, right? I am sure Mr. Hendo will be able to give you a job there."

"No child," said Mr. Luke. "Hendo Enterprises is not the place for Liam."

"But you have worked there, what is it like Mr. Luke?" asked Floza.

"Floza, sit down child," said Mr. Luke, so she sat on the sofa next to Mr. Luke's bed.

"Who better than me to tell you about Hendo Enterprises. I have worked for Hendo enterprises since I was an eighteen-year-old boy. I was so excited the first day I started at Hendo Enterprises, it was the biggest enterprise in Durbey. The owner Mr. Hendo had many other enterprises in Durbey, but this was the biggest. I worked as an apprentice in the laboratory. It was challenging at first but I grew to like it. All was well, until things started changing for the worst. It did not turn out to be as enjoyable as we thought it would be."

"Why is that?" asked Floza.

"As we started doing our jobs very well, we worked on inventing many things to make the city better, and it was a good cause that we worked for. It was because of Mr. Hendo and his bright ideas that we created a beautiful city. That was until Mr. Hendo changed. He grew greedy, worked against his friends to get to the top. He wanted power and he wanted it by all means," said Mr. Luke.

"What's he like, I mean Mr. Hendo?" asked Floza. "Mr. Hendo is a very tall man, he always wears a suit and a top hat on his head. He is a brilliant man, a scientist, inventor and great magician. Magic is something that was created by unnatural means to gain power, Mr. Hendo searched the world for it, until he found one of the greatest magicians of all times, Master Gillians. It was from Master Gillians that he learnt to cast spells and then he came up with a great idea to use this in his experiments. Master Gillians passed away, but Mr. Hendo was the successor of his work and so he built on it, and used it not the way Master Gillians would have intended it to be used. Don't get me wrong, Mr. Hendo's inventions were out of this world, but he uses his brilliance and money to hurt and manipulate people. In fact, not just people, he started doing experiments on animals, mainly cats. He was fascinated that they had nine lives and so he wanted to make a race of people that had the same features as cats."

"Cat people?" asked Floza.

"Yes child, Cat people," replied Mr. Luke.

"He called them 'Conploys', as they were bound by a life-long contract to work for Mr. Hendo. The millionaires of the world would place orders with Mr. Hendo to invent new machines, sometimes spells to improve their enterprises. Eventually Mr. Hendo started casting spells on his contracts of labor, where his employees were bonded by a lifelong contract to Hendo Enterprises."

"What is a lifelong contract Mr. Luke? Did this mean that Mr. Hendo did not allow his employees to ever leave?" asked Floza.

"You are quite correct Floza, the employees of Hendo Enterprises were bound, it was only upon death that the employees would be released, only when the employee passed on was the spell broken.

The employees committed their lives to work for Mr. Hendo, in fact they didn't have a choice. They did not get many holidays, worked long hours and did not spend much time with their families. It was as if Mr. Hendo owned these employees, he gave slavery a new name," explained Mr. Luke.

"Why did these people agree to work for Mr. Hendo knowing they would be bound to him for life?" asked Floza.

"Well, they did not have much of a choice. There were not many enterprises in Durbey. In fact, Durbey was a small town until Mr. Hendo started developing the place, he built tall buildings, opened new enterprises as the years went by," went on Mr. Luke.

"In fact, my father is also bonded by a lifelong contract with Mr. Hendo," said Liam.

"All his workers are bound to him, this can never be broken. His contracts are locked with many spells, which are very difficult to break."

"But your father is in no condition to work, Liam? How will he go back to Hendo Enterprises?" asked Floza.

"We will talk about that later," said Liam.

"Oh no Floza," said Mr. Luke. "Mr. Hendo will not allow me to stay at home even though I am in this condition. He will order his 'Conploys' to come for me and if I refuse, he will not spare me."

"You mean, he would actually ...." Floza's voice trailed off.

"Kill me, yes," confirmed Mr. Luke. Liam stormed out of the room crying, after hearing his father's words. He himself knew that Mr. Hendo was too powerful to defeat and his father's life was in Mr. Hendo's hands.

"Wait Liam," yelled Mr. Luke. He had realized that he had said a bit too much, but this was the reality of the situation.

"I am so sorry, Mr. Luke," said Floza. "I had no idea that working for Mr. Hendo destroyed your entire life. I am quite shocked listening to all these bad things Mr. Hendo has done and is doing. I think coming here has answered a lot of my questions."

"Namely one," she thought. "Stacy is a 'Conploy', and so are all the women in the hostel. She lied to me, when all this time she was working for Mr. Hendo. It makes sense now. When Alice mentioned that Mr. Stevens is no more, and the 'Cherry on Top' no longer exists.

"Mr. Luke, I will take leave now. It was great meeting you and please take care," said Floza.

"Thank you for coming Floza, please speak to Liam before you leave. He needs a friend," said Mr. Luke.

Floza could not believe all that she heard about Mr. Hendo, most of all she was stunned that Stacy was in fact a 'Conploy', a mere experiment of Mr. Hendo. She stepped outside the cottage, only to find Liam sobbing in the front yard. She did not know what to say to him, after all there was not much she could do to change the situation.

"I will try to help him, as much as I can," thought Floza.

"Floza, Oh Floza," sobbed Liam. "This is just horrible. My father is going to die if he goes back to work at Hendo Enterprises and there is nothing I can do to help him. I am so helpless right now," said Liam. Floza tried to comfort him, she was actually very bad at this, but she was a friend that offered guidance and tried to support how she could.

"I would trade places with him any day," said Liam. "I am sure you would, I would do the same for my father," replied Floza.

"Trade places," repeated Liam.

"That's it Floza. I think I found a way to save my father. Promise you'll help me," asked Liam.

"But how Liam?" asked Floza. "You just said there was nothing you could do to help."

"Not if... I trade places with my father," replied Liam. "You mean....?" questioned Floza.

"Yes Floza. I mean, not if I sign a contract with Mr. Hendo in place of my father," said Liam.

"That will mean you will be bound to Hendo Enterprises for life. You have your entire life ahead of you! No Liam!" exclaimed Floza.

"This is what I have to do Floza. Now promise me you will not say a word to my father until Mr. Hendo accepts my offer," said Liam.

Floza did not like the idea of Liam being bound to Hendo

Enterprises for life, but she had no choice, she had to help her friend.

"I will make an appointment to see Mr. Hendo, will you accompany me Floza?" asked Liam.

"Yes, I will Liam," replied Floza.

"Thank you, this means so much to me," said Liam. "But how will I know when to accompany you?" asked Floza.

"I will call you on the phone at 'Eat Your Heart Out'. I will not give away my name and I will inform you when the appointment is to meet with Mr. Hendo," replied Liam.

"Okay Liam, I will have to leave now, the Durbey Express will be there to fetch me," said Floza.

"I'll walk you," said Liam. "Thank you," replied Floza.

They both walked through the olive trees, it was a beautiful sight. The sun was about to set, and luckily Floza had reached her pick-up spot in time. The Durbey Express was there to fetch her. She hugged Liam goodbye and they parted ways.

CHAPTER 10

THE MAGICAL DOOR

The journey to Olive Place had been quite an experience for Floza. She had learnt so many things that she had not known before visiting Liam and his father Luke. In fact, it was also her encounter with Alice, that had made her curious about Stacy's actual place of work. Floza now had some investigating to do, about Stacy. She did not want to implicate her, but felt she needed to know the truth. After all, she was living in a hostel full of 'Conploys'.

"I wonder if Gracy is a 'Conploy' too," thought Floza. "Her reaction was a bit strange when I tried to open the door, in the bath room."

Stacy walked into the room, all smiles. "Are you ready for breakfast?" asked Stacy.

"I'll be there in a few," replied Floza.

Floza joined Stacy in the dining hall. She had so many questions to ask her, but she felt she needed more information.

"So how is your practice going... for the Durbey Talent show? It is just in a few days," asked Stacy.

"How about we meet later on this evening, we can practice then, Floza? Are you okay?"

"Yes, Stacy I am fine," replied Floza.

"You are very quiet today," asked Stacy.

"Oh, it's nothing. I just have a lot on my mind," replied Floza.

"Sure, we'll meet, later...... this evening. I am leaving for work now. Have a lovely day."

"Same to you Floza," replied Stacy.

Floza always had left the hostel before Stacy, in fact she was the first to leave the hostel every morning, since she had an early shift at 'Eat Your Heart Out'.

But this time Floza did not leave, she had lied to Stacy that she was leaving. She walked back into her room and hid behind her bed, until when the lady cats were ready to leave for work, she heard them giggling as they walked out of their rooms. Then a bell rang, it sounded like a siren.

As soon as the siren rang the lady cats walked off briskly. But not in the direction of the entrance to the hostel. Actually, away from it! Floza tiptoed, so as to not cause a disturbance that could blow her cover. She followed the lady cats as they walked down the hall; they were in fact walking towards the direction of the bath rooms.

"That's strange," thought Floza.

"Why would they walk to the bathrooms?"

"Unless they were going to check their appearance before they left?"

It was seven o clock, and Floza was now late for her shift at 'Eat Your Heart Out'.

"I will have to make up a story to Mr. Charlie."

"Wait a minute, its seven o'clock. How come the cats have not transformed?" she thought.

She recalled the time when Stacy had told her the cat transformation takes place from six o clock in the morning to six o clock in the evening. So why had they not transformed? all the lady cats were now in the bathroom, she could hear them. There was a little spacing left at the bathroom door, and it gave Floza just enough space to peek inside.

The lady cats seemed to be standing behind the very same door she had tried to unlock the day before…they stood in a line, until the door opened. It seemed to have opened from the other side. The door remained opened until each lady cat had walked in, Stacy was also in line. Where could they be going? More importantly, who was on the other side of the door? Just as the last lady cat walked through the door, the door shut!

"Oh no, I'm too late!" thought Floza.

"How do I get to see what's on the other side?"

"I will have to try and open this door myself, but I have to check if Gracy is near or else I will be in trouble!"

So she went outside the bathroom, to check if the coast was clear.

It was! "Now to open this door," said Floza.

She pulled the door open with all her might, and when it opened, there was a beam of light radiating from it…there was no one on the other side.

"But…. there must be something on the other side," thought Floza.

"Maybe… if I walk through the door I will find out?"

So she walked through the door. It was if she was walking through a tunnel of light, until she came to a room. The room looked like a ladies dressing room. There were many cupboards labelled with numbers. It was not a fancy room, just a basic change room. There was no one inside the change room, at least for a while….

"This must be the place where the lady cats change," thought Floza. "But where did they go to now….? Is it safe to venture out further into this place? Well I won't know unless I try."

She walked away from the change rooms until she came to a hallway; there were arrows pointing in both directions. To the right was the production line and to the left was the laboratory.

"Could it be that I am inside?" she thought. Just as she was about to choose her direction, she heard someone walking down the hall. The footsteps sounded as if they were approaching the change room. Floza panicked, she did not know which direction to go, so she hurried back to the change rooms.

"These Conploys are filthy, see to it that you clean this change room," requested a voice.

"Yes, Sir Mugbie," replied another voice.

"Mugbie? Who is Mugbie?" thought Floza.

"Oh, and Sir Mugbie, would you perhaps know when Mr. Hendo will be back from his expedition?" asked the voice.

"What would you need that information for?" asked Mugbie.

"Sir, I needed to clean his suits, they need to be ready for him on his return," replied the Conploy.

"Oh, his suits…" said Mugbie.

"Yes, Sir Mugbie," replied the Conploy.

"It was a special request that all Mr. Hendo suits be cleaned at the laundry."

"See to it that it is done before his arrival tomorrow," said Mugbie.

"I will make sure of it," replied the Conploy. "Mr. Hendo?" thought Floza.

"Could it be that I am inside Hendo Enterprises? All this time the lady cats were using this magical door to come into Hendo Enterprises. So, this is where Stacy really works..."

Mugbie had left the change rooms and the Conploy remained to clean, as he had requested. Floza was terrified of getting caught, she needed to get back to the door without the "Conploy" seeing.

"How do I get pass this Conploy, I need to create a distraction of some kind," she thought.

She found an umbrella hanging from the locker. She picked it up and threw it in the direction of the door, to cause a disturbance. The Conploy heard the sound outside the door and went outside to check if someone was there.

"That's strange, I thought something had fallen," said the Conploy.

Just as he turned his back, Floza opened the magical door and stormed through it, "Phew, that was close," she thought.

The Conploy walked back into the change room, only to find that the magical door, leading to Eva's women's hostel, was open.

"I do not recall seeing this door opened, the lady cats can be so careless at times," he said.

The Conploy then closed the door, and the gateway between both places closed, at least for now. Floza could not believe what had just happened. The magical door that she had just discovered in the hostel was a gateway to Hendo Enterprises. She had no idea that such a simple hostel could have hidden mysterious secrets.

"I am certain that Gracy's aware of this," thought Floza.

"For all I know she is also a worker of Mr. Hendo. What puzzle's me though, is the reason Edor directed me to this specific hostel, which is in fact a commune for Conploys. I will have to head back to work right away before Mr. Charlie notices I am not there."

Floza tried to occupy herself at work; even though she had so many dishes to wash and customers to see, all she could think about was about the truth about Eva's women's home, Stacy and the Conploys.

"Floza, there is a call for you!" said Mr. Charlie.

"It's your cousin, Sam, he wants to speak to you, he says it's quite urgent."

"Cousin Sam," thought Floza. "Oh yes, it must be Liam. He did say he was not going to mention his name." "Thanks Mr. Charlie, I will take the call right away,"
replied Floza.

The telephone was situated in Mr. Charlie's office; it was a bit chaotic in there with all the paper lying around. Floza walked towards the desk, to answer the telephone. "Hello, this is Floza," she said.

"Hello, Floza. This is Liam…. how are you?" "I am good Liam, thank you," replied Floza.

"I called to inform you that I have got an appointment to see Mr. Hendo, tomorrow," said Liam.

"I know this is short notice, but I hope that you have not changed your mind about accompanying me?"

"No Liam, I have not changed my mind. I have so much to tell you," said Floza. "Where shall we meet tomorrow?"

"We shall meet outside the Durbey Theater, we will walk to Hendo Enterprises from there," replied Liam.

"Meet you at ten o clock tomorrow in the morning." "Okay Liam see you tomorrow. Goodbye, for now," said Floza.

Later that day, Floza thought about how she was going to confront Stacy about everything she had seen in the morning. She waited in her room until Stacy arrived from Hendo

Enterprises. She had heard the chitter chatter of the lady cats coming from the hallway; they had returned to the hostel. Stacy entered the room to find Floza sitting on her bed.

"You're home early," asked Stacy.

"My shift at the restaurant finished a bit early, replied Floza.

"Is that so? Aren't you lucky? I had a rough day at work, Mr. Stevens was in such a foul mood today. We had so many cake orders, it was never ending..."

"Are you sure you don't mean Mugbie, Stacy," asked Floza.

"Whatever do you mean Floza? I have never heard of that name before," replied Stacy.

"Please stop lying Stacy, I saw everything this morning," said Floza.

Stacy was stunned that Floza had mentioned Mugbie's name. She tried to hide her feelings of guilt, but the expression on her face clearly showed that she was guilty about something.

"What did you see this morning Floza?" asked Stacy. "It seems that it has made you very upset."

"I trusted you!" said Floza. "I know that you do not work for Mr. Stevens, you work for Mr. Hendo!"

"Errr......err..." Stacy hesitated. She did not know how to respond to what Floza had just said.

"I saw you, and the other cat ladies, walking through the magic door. Behind that door is none other than Hendo Enterprises. I know the truth Stacy! You are a 'Conploy', an experiment of Mr. Hendo Wallens. I know everything! You cannot lie to me anymore! This hostel is a commune for 'Conploys'," said Floza in a rather angry tone.

She was very upset after finding out the truth. She had trusted Stacy, and after finding out that Stacy was in fact a 'Conploy' she felt betrayed.

"I am so sorry Floza," signed Stacy.

"I wanted to tell you the truth," but I was too scared. Mr. Hendo swore that if we told anyone about this, if we exposed ourselves in anyway, he would not spare us. We have never left Eva's Hostel, at least only for a short while. When you started living at the hostel it was the beginning of the experiment, hence you saw my human form. However now… I cannot transform to my human self; the experiment is now complete. I will never be human again," said Stacy in a very sad tone.

"Why did you allow Mr. Hendo to experiment on you?" asked Floza.

"I did not have a choice," replied Stacy. "You see my mother Florence was an employee at Hendo Enterprises, she was not just any employee but a great scientist. She worked directly under Mr. Hendo. I was so proud of her."

"Was proud of her?" asked Floza.

"Yes," signed Stacy. "She is no more. My mother died fighting for a good cause. That is how I like to remember her."

"What was the cause Stacy?" asked Floza.

"My mother stood up to Mr. Hendo when she learned that his experiments with animals and humans were out of control. Mr. Hendo eventually started experimenting on his own employees. That is the reason my mother stood up to him," replied Stacy.

"Why on earth would Mr. Hendo experiment on his own employees?" asked Floza.

"Mr. Hendo is a wicked, wicked man, Floza. He manipulated the natural order of life, to entertain himself and to make his enterprise more profitable. It was all about the money and profits from his experiments. Everything Mr. Hendo did was not for the good of the people, it was always to make himself more rich and powerful. Mr. Hendo conjured his spells in the craftiest ways to ensure that his secrets would stay well protected, but at a huge price to the human race. So being a cat at that time was not really my choice, Floza. After my mother died, Mr. Hendo took me in as a guinea-pig for his experiments. I am only a scientific experiment of Mr. Hendo, I will never be my normal human self again," signed Stacy.

"Stacy, I had no idea, that you were an experiment, until I entered the magical door," said Floza.

"There must be a way for you to become your human self again?"

"I am sure Mr. Hendo can use some of his magic or science to change you back to normal," said Floza.

"Maybe he can Floza…, but I don't think he would," said Stacy.

"Why not Stacy?" asked Floza.

"Mr. Hendo is a very bad man, he would never allow for his 'Conploys' to leave Hendo Enterprises. I signed the magic contract and pledged just like all the other 'Conploys' to work for Hendo Enterprises for life."

"We are all bound to him now, the contract will never be broken."

"I don't understand, why Mr. Hendo would bind his employees to a magic contract," replied Floza. "Is it not enough that he is the wealthiest and most powerful man in Durbey?"

"That is not enough for him, Floza. You see years ago when Mr. Hendo had just built Hendo Enterprises, he had a number of people working for him, but then they left one by one," said Stacy.

"Why did they leave Hendo Enterprises?" asked Floza. "These employees were not happy with the way Mr. Hendo treated them, they also started noticing Mr.

Hendo conducting experiments that were harmful to people and animals."

127

"Eventually the employees who resigned reported Mr. Hendo to the Board of enterprises, which governed the businesses in the world. Once this information leaked out Hendo Enterprises was on the verge of being exposed to the Board of Enterprises. Mr. Hendo was called to the Board of Enterprises to state his testimony in the case. He did this so well that the board of enterprises ended up doing absolutely nothing about Mr. Hendo or the injustices that took place at Hendo Enterprises."

"How is this possible? You mentioned that the Board of Enterprises were overseeing all the enterprises in the world. Why did they ignore what Mr. Hendo was doing?" asked Floza.

"Mr. Hendo conjured a spell with the help of Master Gillian's magic book; he created a spell that was so powerful that it would convince the Board to change their minds about persecuting him. And so ever since, he has done anything he could possibly do to ensure that his enterprises grow larger and his profits become more and more. Obviously, this was at a price; Mr. Hendo eventually lost his close friends, and in fact he turned them into his enemies. His friends betrayed him by stealing the book of magic, which contained all the knowledge of spells. The spell of 'containment' cast on the Board of Enterprises, will soon fade off unless Mr. Hendo finds his magic book. So, he has relied on science to create 'Conploys' and invented machines that will assist him in his crafty schemes," said Stacy.

"I do hope that he never finds that book again. All of the 'Conploys' will be free," said Floza.

"But if he does.... we are bound to him for life," replied Stacy.

CHAPTER 11

INSIDE HENDO ENTERPRISES

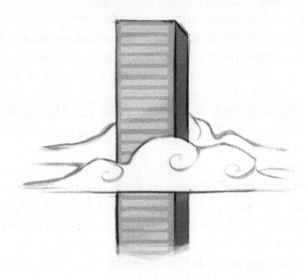

"Sweet seeing my old friend Loops, it's been years," said Mr. Hendo. "He hasn't aged but then again I look ravishing for my age."

He begins to sing as he travels away from Clobet Valley:

"I am sailing in a blue sea
it's taking me, waves are taking me
to the place of hidden mystery
was friends but now Foe
in time they will know…"

Mr. Hendo sang in a high-pitched voice, he mostly made up the words as he sang along. He was travelling in the teleporting bubble back to Durbey; he was quite proud of the act he had pulled off at Clobet Valley. After this mysterious act, as the strange man, he knew that he had stirred something up, some doubt and questions among the elders of the Valley.

"I know the way Loops thinks; he will definitely know something is out of place," he thought.

"I'll give him some time to 'itch a bit'. He can roll about in curiosity and doubt. It will make me so happy to watch that."

"Oh! I might have to get some scenes recorded for me to watch. I will have to ask Mugbie, my scientist, to make sure my looking glass is working."

The looking glass was an invention that Mr. Hendo had created to spy on people and their whereabouts at any place or time.

"I'll be back at Clobet Valley soon," said Mr. Hendo.

"I have so much of work to finish before I complete my mission. The easiest part is over, which was luring Floza into Durbey, the girl was so easy to convince. But she could not help it seeing her father so ill. Now comes the part when I revenge those who have betrayed me and Hendo Enterprises. They won't know what hit them, they thought building this new place, Clobet Valley, would protect them forever. I am a powerful man, they know this as well, I have access to all sorts of inventions they can only dream of making. Nevertheless, today a few drops of rain are falling on my friends at Clobet Valley. Let the thunder storm begin, and when the storm begins not even your friendship will save you from my wrath," said Mr. Hendo as he started laughing an evil laugh.

The bubble eventually reached Durbey; it landed on a tall building which was more like a skyscraper. It was over ninety floors high and it was illuminated with purple and blue lights. At the very top of the building was a sign called Hendo Enterprises. This building was the very same building that Floza had seen the day she landed in Durbey.

"Aaahhh!!"

"Home sweet home," said Mr. Hendo. "My magnificent home, the most outstanding!! building in Durbey. In fact, one of my most outstanding buildings in Durbey."

"Activate face recognition," said Mr. Hendo.

"Face scanned," said the robot scanner, "Access allowed into Hendo Enterprises."

"Good Evening Mr. Hendo, I hope you had a good flight."

"Why thank you Face recognition 2000!" said Mr. Hendo, "You are still one of my most prized inventions." "Ha, ha, ha, ha, ha, ha, ha, ha," laughed the robot.

"Thank you, Sir."

"Soon will come the day where we will do away with the weakling humans," said Mr. Hendo.

"So far, my animal studies are going quite nicely, not so well for my guinea pigs though, ha, ha. Those cat ladies were kind enough to volunteer for my new experiment. They just wanted money, and I paid them, because I have so much of it! Their cat genes will definitely make them stronger workers! Cats have nine lives, now humans have ten!! Imagine how we could use these species to better my Enterprise. The world will want my new species of workers. Construction, mining, the military, there is no limit for the use of this species. Goodbye humans!!"

Mr. Hendo Wallens entered the building and it sure was a sight to see! The rooms were furnished to perfection, the walls were high and the ceilings of the rooms were covered with glossy matter that moved in motion. It was like a spell was cast on the ceilings to give it the effect of the universe.

Each room had a number of machines and inventions that made it quite effortless for Mr. Hendo to do things for himself. His inventions were magnificent!! He did not need many employees to assist him, nor did he need a cook– his machines did absolutely everything!

"Cup of Coffee," requested Mr. Hendo. "Espresso or Latte, for you?" replied a robot.

"Latte! I need to relax after my tiring adventure to Clobet Valley."

"Would you care to put your feet up?" said another voice.

"Yes, actually I would," said Mr. Hendo.

"I need a bath and a change of suit, and call for Mugbie once I'm done!"

"We have some catching up to do!"

"Your bath water is ready," said the robot. "It will be at the exact temperature you desire."

"37 degrees Celsius," asked Mr. Hendo.

"Yes Mr. Hendo, just as your body temperature," said the robot.

"Magnificent!! Well-done. Now get me my suit, I need to change into something fresh," said Mr. Hendo.

"Mugbie is at the door!" said the robot.

"Give me a minute, I am still doing my hair, robot," said Mr. Hendo.

"I thought you named me Tim, Mr. Hendo?" asked the robot.

"You are not worthy of a name yet, so I shall call you Robot," replied Mr. Hendo.

"Oh, my life, my life," said the robot.

"You don't have a life," said Mr. Hendo. "Now I will meet Mugbie in the meeting room. Bring us some of that gonog juice, the one from France."

"You mean Gognog, Sir," replied the robot. "Just get me the juice!" shouted Mr. Hendo. "Right away," replied the robot.

Mugbie was Mr. Hendo's main scientist. He managed his laboratories while Mr. Hendo was away on his crafty adventures, and trust me Mr. Hendo had many of those. Mugbie was a short man, he wore a lab coat and he had the strangest hair. It always stuck up in the air as if he had been electrocuted. In fact, Mugbie had been electrocuted, it was at a time, a time no one would forget. Many years ago, the laboratories of Hendo enterprises were destroyed, in an explosion. Mr. Hendo was devastated but then he instructed Mugbie and the other scientists to build the laboratory once again.

"You called for me, Sir?" asked Mugbie

"Why would I be here if I had not called for you, Mugbie?" replied Mr. Hendo.

"But enough of my sarcasm, I needed to see you, there are some urgent matters at hand. I want you Mugbie, to restore my looking glass. I need it for some urgent work. See to it that this is done immediately. I…. have found them Mugbie."

"Found who, Sir?" asked Mugbie. "My old friends," replied Mr. Hendo.

"Them, are you serious? But I thought they were dead?"

"No, they escaped Mugbie, to a place they thought we could never find them," said Mr. Hendo. "Soon we will revenge those who have caused your hair to look dreadful twenty-four seven."

"Sir, please don't make my hair a joke," said Mugbie. "My wife has not been happy with me ever since the incident."

"I can't imagine how she could be happy, Mugbie when you are looking the way you do. I would love to see our old friends, or should I say enemies defeated!!"

"What about the book Sir, have you found it?" asked Mugbie.

"Not as yet Mugbie, but I will soon. After Loops realizes his daughter was captured by me, he will bring it back to me. Loops will beg for mercy, he will obey me!" yelled Mr. Hendo.

"Sir, I will see to it that the looking glass is in order," said Mugbie.

"Would you care for some, Gognog juice?" asked the robot.

"No none for me," replied Mugbie.

"You must try some Gognog juice, Mugbie. I tried it in France during one of my expeditions. Tim pour us some Gognog juice," said Mr. Hendo.

"But sir, you said I do not the deserve the name Tim," replied the robot.

"I can call you as I please, now leave robot," said Mr. Hendo.

"It is rather good Sir" said Mugbie.

"I must say Mugbie, your teleporting bubble is one off the best inventions you have made thus far," said Mr. Hendo.

"Thank you, Sir," said Mugbie. "I am glad you are finding good use for it."

"Oh, trust me Mugbie, I am indeed making full use of the teleporting bubble. In fact, I want you to make one more," said Mr. Hendo.

"What for Mr. Hendo?" asked Mugbie.

"The Durbey Fair. I gave my word to sponsor a prize for the Durbey Talent show. I was thinking… I either go large or go home for the prize sponsorship. I think the teleporting bubble will be the best prize anyone has ever sponsored to the people of Durbey. One lucky contestant will be winning the bubble. That person will be the luckiest person indeed," said Mr. Hendo.

"But Sir, why not sponsor something smaller like a looking glass, or…" said Mugbie.

"Did you not hear me? Mugbie?" replied Mr. Hendo in a cheeky voice.

"I want to go large! Now see to it that you create a new bubble, before the Annual Durbey Fair. Use one of those cat people in you laboratory to do a trial. We cannot sponsor a prize that does not work to the people of Durbey. That would be disastrous," said Mr. Hendo.

"Sir are you saying that you care about the people of Durbey?" asked Mugbie.

"No, of course I do not care about the people of Durbey, I care about my reputation," said Mr. Hendo.

"Sir, I forgot to mention just one thing. One of the 'Conploys' passed on while working on the production line. His nine lives had run out," replied Mugbie.

"Was it the same Conploy that was sent to the military?" asked Mr. Hendo.

"Yes Mr. Hendo, Sir."

"I am surprised he lasted that long. See to it that his family is informed, and make sure that you replace his position immediately. We can't have my production suffer, just because of the death of one weakling Conploy," said Mr. Hendo.

"Yes sir, I will see to it that the position is filled immediately," replied Mugbie.

"Soon we won't have to rely on humans, when the cat workers are developed and running. All my workers will have ten lives, there will be no need for humans again!! Ha, Ha, Ha," laughed Mr. Hendo.

"Yes Sir, no more humans at Hendo Enterprises. I will leave now, I will deliver your requests on time," said Mugbie.

"See to it that you do," replied Mr. Hendo. He then got up from his fancy couch, lifted his nose in the air, and walked away to his quarters.

"Sir Mugbie!" called a person walking through the laboratory. He was short, furry, and resembled a cat. He was one of the cat people experimented on at Hendo Laboratories.

"What do you want? Conploy, you should be at the production line at this hour," said Mugbie.

"How dare you leave the production line without permission?"

"It is rather urgent, Sir Mugbie... is it true that some off my kind are going to be exported to other parts of the world? I need to know, I have family just like you," said the Conploy.

"Family!!!! I have a wife and she is all the family I can handle! Yes, it's true, some of you Conploys are going to be exported to Asia; there is a massive project that you will be working on for Hendo Enterprises," replied Mugbie.

"Project? What kind of project?" asked the Conploy. "I cannot say much about it, but it does involve working under dangerous conditions. So we agreed to outsource you Conploys, since you have nine lives it won't be an issue now will it? Plus we make lots of money. When Mr. Hendo is happy with my work, all is well," said Mugbie trying to justify to the Conploy that he was working for a good cause.

"What happens.... when our nine lives run out?" asked the Conploy.

"Then you have one more, your human life! Aren't you lucky to have ten lives? Why... if I were as lucky as you, I would make the most of all my lives," said Mugbie.

"But we are not human anymore and we are not animal either," said the Conploy. The Conploy sounded as if he was in agonizing pain. "What have you created? Can you not see that we feel pain when our claws are so long? When there is hair growing in our ears, and when our chests are burdened with hair balls?"

"I promise to create better Conploys without the bad effects of the animal," replied Mugbie. "Now get back to work."

So the Conploy followed Mugbie's instructions and returned to his duties.

Meanwhile Mr. Hendo, was busy following up on his affairs at Hendo Enterprises, since he had just returned from his expedition. Mr. Hendo called for his secretary, Mrs. Gladess, who was his right-hand organizer and planner at the enterprise.

Gladess was a very mature lady, she had a long face and the design of her spectacles were very strange, they looked rather pointy at the ends. Gladess made sure that she was always dressed professionally, as she represented the face of Hendo Enterprises.

"Gladess is at the door," said the robot.

"I am ready," replied Mr. Hendo.

Gladess walked into Mr. Hendo's office. It was a large room filled with different ornaments and gadgets. At the very top of the wall was a picture of Mr. Hendo himself, wearing a top hat and holding a walking stick, whilst posing eloquently.

"Good Morning," said Gladess. Her voice was very coarse; it sounded much like a man's voice. In fact, Gladess always wore pant suits, and she was very masculine in her mannerisms.

"Come in Gladess, and take a seat," replied Mr. Hendo.

"How was your trip, Mr. Hendo Sir?" asked Gladess.

"It was quite productive, more productive than I thought it would be," said Mr. Hendo as he laughed.

"Now do update me on what has transpired, while I was away."

"Sir, Mr. Vogati would like to meet with you tomorrow, he has a special request from Hendo Enterprises," said Gladess.

"Mr. Vogati, you say? He's a business owner from another country, am I right?" asked Mr. Hendo.

"Yes Sir, you are right, he mentioned something about Conploys to be outsourced for the mines in Calcutta," said Gladess.

"Yes I remember, Gladess, make a booking with him for tomorrow afternoon, I am looking forward to doing business with Mr. Vogati. He is going to be the first from all other businesses to use my Conploys," said Mr. Hendo.

"That is great Sir! I am glad that your project is taking off successfully. There is also a request from a boy named Liam. He requested to meet with you today at two o'clock. I put him down for this time – I hope you do not mind," asked Gladess.

"Liam, who is he?" asked Mr. Hendo.

"He mentioned that he is the son of an employee who works here, and he needs to meet with you as a matter of urgency," replied Gladess.

"What is this regarding? I have no time for employee's issues," stormed Hendo.

"I don't know Sir...., he mentioned that he will discuss this, with you on his return. He did speak of a contract," said Gladess.

"A contract you say? I see now... he would like to work for Hendo Enterprises. I don't blame him, Hendo Enterprises is the most successful and renowned in the world! Sure! I'll see this boy Lee," said Mr. Hendo.

"Liam Sir," said Gladess as she corrected Mr. Hendo. Today was the day that Liam was to meet Mr. Hendo for the first time, Floza was to escort him to Hendo Enterprises, and the reason for this visit was to discuss Mr. Luke's condition. Liam had been lucky enough to get an appointment with Mr. Hendo; normally Mr. Hendo did not have much time for people matters.

CHAPTER 12

THE PICTURE ON THE WALL

Floza woke up early that morning to prepare herself for the visit at Hendo Enterprises. She had reported to Mr. Charlie that she was unwell and needed the day off; he was not very happy about this. However, Mr. Charlie could not do much about her staying away due to illness. Liam was a special friend to her, and she felt that staying away from work just for a day was a small sacrifice to make.

"Good Morning Floza," said Stacy.

"I see you are still in your sleepwear. Are you not heading to work today?"

"Well Stacy, I am not feeling too well, so I took the day off," replied Floza. "I think some bed rest will do me some good."

"Maybe you need to visit the doctor?" asked Stacy. "No, I think I just need to relax a bit today," replied Floza.

Floza obviously was not really sick, but she had to lie to Stacy; accompanying Liam to Hendo Enterprises was a secret just between Liam and herself.

"Well then, I hope you get well soon. I am off to work. We will meet at dinner time," said Stacy.

"Floza, please take it easy today, I know I have put you through a lot of stress as well. I lied and I feel really bad about it, and Floza, I hope you haven't changed your mind about taking part in the Durbey Talent Show?"

"No Stacy, I have not changed my mind, I am still looking forward to winning the teleporting bubble. I will start practice from tomorrow, and we can decide on my costume, since the talent show is only three days away. I don't have much time to practice."

Floza had felt very nervous, she was not prepared enough to perform at the Durbey Talent show.

"Don't worry Floza," said Stacy as she patted Floza gently on the back.

"We will have you prepared by tomorrow night. Take care then," she said, and she left with the other cat ladies to head to Hendo Enterprises."

Meanwhile, Liam was on his way to the Durbey theater, where he was to meet Floza. The Durbey Theater always attracted a crowd, since the people of Durbey loved entertainment. Outside stood a ticket booth, which attracted crowds of people. The theater was a popular spot for the wealthy, it was used as a social scene for the rich and elite. It was very much a scene of fashion for the people of Durbey, well at least for those who could afford spending their money on useless garments.

"Tonight's show, the release of Mr. Hendo's 'workforce apocalypse'," a man announced.

"Mr. Hendo involved in theatre, who would have guessed?" thought Liam.

"I wonder what the 'workforce apocalypse' is about? Sounds like Mr. Hendo is starting a revolution of some kind. Now… where could Floza be? It's past ten o'clock. Oh well, she is probably running a bit late."

Indeed she was, Floza walked briskly in the streets of Durbey town. She walked through crowds of people, who were on their way to places of work. She so happened to pass a boutique, which was called Bedazzle.

Something in the window caught her eye; it was the most perfect costume for the Durbey Talent show, an electric green leotard, with bell sleeves and silver lining as the ends.

"This is perfect!" thought Floza. "I will surely be noticed if I could wear this for the Durbey Talent Show." So she decided to visit the store Bedazzle, it was a big store with all sorts of fancy costumes and accessories. But there seemed to be no one inside, so Floza walked towards the counter as she noticed a bell of some sort.

She reached for the bell and pressed it once tring… tring…, still no answer.

She pressed it twice: tring, tring, at last a response, a women peeked from behind a long curtain, at the back of the store.

"Hold on, I'll be with you in a minute," she said.

Floza patiently waited for her as she walked to the front of the store, so as to attend to her. She looked like a gypsy in her long dress, and her hair was tied back in a shiny sort of cloth. The lady seemed friendly as she smiled; when she noticed Floza standing in front of the store, she also had a strong presence, like she was a women of strong spirit.

"Good Morning to you, welcome to Bedazzle. I am Gertha, the owner of this bedazzling store. How can I help you this fine morning?"

"Good Morning Miss," replied Floza as she smiled back at the lady.

"I was walking past your store, when I noticed an outfit on that plastic person? I thought it would be perfect for the show I will be taking part in."

"You mean the mannequin," laughed Gertha. "Point out which costume has caught your eye."

Floza pointed to the mannequin dressed in the green leotard.

"Oh I see," said Gertha as she walked towards the mannequin. "Do come closer girl."

"My name is Floza," said Floza. The lady paused for a moment, and then she replied, whilst starring at Floza. "What a pretty name. Whereabout in Durbey are you from?"

"I am from the city," replied Floza.

"So am I," she replied, smiling at Floza without actually blinking.

"Oh! I almost forgot, it's the costume that you came in for; this is a dancer's costume."

"Yes, I am a dancer Miss Gertha," said Floza.

"Is that so... so was I in my younger days, but I was too boyish to continue with my ballet classes. My father grew tired of me skipping my lessons. It was his dream you know, for me to be a ballet dancer, but my mind was more curious about other things. Enough about me," she said.

Gertha took out the costume from the mannequin, it was indeed a stunning costume, it had many diamonds sewn on the detail, not real diamonds of course.

"The bling is just bedazzling," said Gertha. "Bling?" asked Floza.

"Yes, the bling, bling, as they say these days, I mean the diamond studs Floza," said Gertha.

"Oh yes, the diamond studs are so pretty, I would love to try this out. But before I get my hopes high, how much for this costume Miss Gertha?" asked Floza.

"You are quite lucky; it is actually on sale, see I am clearing all my old garments and bringing in new ones. This garment will be ten silvers," said Gertha.

"Oh... ten silvers," replied Floza in a rather disappointed tone.

She did not have ten silvers to spend on her costume for the talent show. It was not as if she earned a lot at 'Eat your heart out', she merely had enough to pay for her hostel fee, but considering the circumstances she had managed to save seven silvers.

"I have changed my mind about trying it on," she said.

"But you like this costume, don't you?" asked Gertha. "I can see it in your eyes; you think it's the one."

"Yes... but Miss Gertha, I don't have ten silvers to buy this costume, I would be wasting your time if I tried it on," said Floza sadly.

"Don't be silly, we'll see what we can do," Gertha said. She was a pleasant lady, Miss Gertha. "So, tell me more, why are you buying this costume?"

"I am taking part in the Durbey Talent show," replied Floza. "I will be doing a dance item, a fusion between ballet and electro music."

"The Durbey Talent show, why that is marvelous. Now please try it on, I am dying to see how it looks on you," smiled Gertha.

So Floza tried on the leotard. It fitted perfectly, the color was very bright and catchy, but she remembered the advice that Stacy had given her about looking like a firework on stage.

"You look beautiful," said Gertha as her eyes lit up. "You are going to make a very pretty ballerina. I have just the pair of shoes that would go perfectly with this. I will be back in a minute."

Gertha went to the back of the store, and came out with a pair of ballet shoes. But not just any ballet shoes, the most stunning silver ballet shoes, covered in glittering diamantes.

"These are so beautiful," said Floza. "I have never seen such exquisite shoes in my life."

"Go ahead. Try them on," said Gertha. She was very excited about Floza's costume.

"Actually, how much are these?" asked Floza. "These shoes are ten silvers," replied Gertha.

"Ten plus ten, that's twenty silvers. O they are really beautiful, but I cannot afford them Miss Gertha."

"Floza…. you are going to be a participant in one of the biggest events in the whole of Durbey." Gertha now extended her hands to place them on Floza's shoulders, and looked down at her." She then went on to say, "The whole of Durbey will be watching you on television; this is your moment, I see you as my own child."

"Do you have any children of your own?" asked Floza. "I used to," she replied. She looked rather down. "But enough about me, I will give you the costume and shoes for five silvers. I want you to look your best for the Durbey Talent show, I will feel so proud that my costumes are on stage. That is enough for me, money is not everything. Floza, when you win the talent show, please don't forget to mention that you picked your costume from Bedazzle, a little online marketing will be good for the business."

"O Gertha, are you sure?" asked Floza. "Yes dear, I am certain," replied Gertha.

Floza paid Gertha the five silvers which was a very, very large discount. She was lucky that Gertha was such a nice lady; there was something similar about them both, which made them feel connected. Floza did not have a lot of time to chat. Liam was waiting for her patiently outside the Durbey Theatre.

"Gertha. What a nice name," thought Floza.

"She seems so familiar, I am so glad I met her and now I have my costume for the talent show. I cannot wait to show Stacy my costume. She is going to be so excited. I could have not had possibly afforded such a glamorous costume, but Gertha was so nice. I have to come back and thank here after the Talent Show. Oh my goodness, its past ten already, Liam will be waiting. I have to hurry…"

Floza walked to the Durbey Theater, until she saw Liam waiting outside. He was looking at his watch, after all her stop at Bedazzle had taken some time.

"Liam is going to be so upset with me," she thought.

"Liam, Liam," she called, while crossing the street to the Durbey Theater.

Liam had heard someone calling his name, and soon he noticed Floza walking towards him. He was really glad to see her, with only fifteen minutes to the appointment, they had to hurry to Hendo Enterprises.

"There you are, I was beginning to think you had changed your mind," said Liam. "But I am sure glad to see you. Come, let's leave at once."

So, both Liam and Floza walked to Hendo Enterprises. It was quite a long walk to Hendo Enterprises; they passed four streets until they came to a river. Behind the river was a huge building.

"This is Hendo Enterprises," said Liam. "It is quite extraordinary is it not?"

Hendo Enterprises was a sure sight to see; the building was so tall it reached into the sky. The walls of the building shone so brightly, since they were made of glass.

"Yes, Liam, it surely is a sight to see," replied Floza. "You should see the building at night. The lights look fantastic," said Liam.

"Actually… I did get a glimpse of it, when I first came to Durbey," replied Floza

Floza thought about the first time she had seen Hendo Enterprises, the very first time Edor had introduced her to Durbey. That seemed like a long time ago.

"To think this is only one of Mr. Hendo's buildings. I wish I were as wealthy as him," moaned Liam.

"You should not wish to be anyone but yourself," said Floza. "Mr. Hendo might have all the money in the world, but he is evil and that is not something to be proud of." "Maybe you are right Floza, but if I were as powerful as Mr. Hendo, I would use my wealth to help people and not exploit them," said Liam.

"You say that now Liam, but it seems this thing called money changes you. I now understand why my father and the elders of the Valley did not introduce money to our society," replied Floza.

"A place without money, are you joking?" questioned Liam.

"No I am not, why would I be joking?" replied Floza. "I did not think that you were lying Floza," said Liam. "I know Liam; it is hard to believe such a place exits, but it does. Now… tell me Liam, how do we get across the river to Hendo Enterprises?" asked Floza.

"There is a ferry that should be coming past this way any moment," replied Liam. "Look there, it is in the distance." It was a small boat, but it moved very quickly; it approached Floza and Liam. The person sailing the boat was a man. He wore a uniform and a captain's hat.

"I am the captain of this ship. Do come in, that will be two silvers to cross to Hendo Enterprises," the captain announced.

"Did he just call this a ship?" laughed Liam.

The sailor was an old man; he seemed quite deranged. "Is this safe?" asked Floza.

"Why sure… it is safe, I am a well experienced sailor. These are calm waters, dear girl. I have sailed on much rougher seas," said the sailor.

"You do know this is a river Sir?" said Liam.

"All rivers lead to the sea, it's the same thing, is it not?" said the sailor.

"Well he does have a point," said Floza as she looked at Liam.

"So, come on board then," said the sailor. They went on-board the boat; it now took off in the direction of Hendo Enterprises. Liam reached for his pocket and placed two silvers in the man's hands.

"So, you both on your way to see Mr. Hendo?" asked the man.

"How did you know?" asked Floza.

"Who else would you visit? After all, no one really goes in to Hendo Enterprises, and those who have gone in, don't really come out," said the sailor.

"Did you hear that Liam…are we walking into a death trap?" asked Floza.

"Calm down Floza, I know what I am doing; besides you are only accompanying me, you will not say a word to Mr. Hendo Wallens," warned Liam.

"Okay Liam, but I am worried for you," said Floza.

"No need to worry about me Floza, I will be just fine," said Liam.

"You have reached your destination!" said the man "Thank you!" said Floza, and both walked off the boat to head towards Hendo Enterprises.

They then came to the entrance of Hendo Enterprises, it was behind a big gate, the gate was engraved with the name

Hendo Enterprises. There was no one to be seen at the entrance, it was so quite without a soul to be seen.

"How do we get past this big gate?" asked Floza.

Liam took a piece of paper out of his pocket; he then noticed a device fixed on the gate and he entered the numbers written on the piece of paper.

"This is a visitor access code that was given to me by Gladess, Mr. Hendo's secretary. As you can see the controls are very much stricter here. Its only Gladess that provides visitors with these codes, once Mr. Hendo has confirmed his appointment, that is."

"Access to Hendo Enterprises denied!" said a voice from the device.

"It seems she has given you the wrong code," replied Floza.

"Wait, let me try once again," said Liam, punching in the numbers once again.

"Access to Hendo Enterprises granted," an electronic voice said.

"I might have missed a digit. Look, the gates are opening."

So, they walked into Hendo Enterprises; as they reached the door Gladess was standing outside, to invite them in.

"I am Gladess, welcome to Hendo Enterprises. Who is this? You did not tell me you were bringing a guest," said Gladess.

"She is my sister," replied Liam. "She is just accompanying me today."

"That might be a problem," said Gladess. "I will need to ask permission from Mr. Hendo before she accompanies you."

Gladess looked at Floza in a strange manner as she was not fond of other women.

"Come in for now," she said to Floza.

There were so many floors in the building. The workers travelled using a glass elevator to get to the different levels of the enterprise. Liam and Floza noticed particularly men and women wearing white laboratory coats, who looked like scientists.

Gladess ordered Floza and Liam to wait in a room whilst she sorted the issue of Floza, being uninvited. It was a very fancy room. Floza decided to take a seat on the couch, to rest a bit.

A voice said to her, "would you like a leg rest?" "This couch just spoke to me," said Floza looking rather confused.

"I heard it too, say something back," replied Liam.

"Yes couch, I would like a leg rest," said Floza. So the couch followed Floza's orders and extended a leg rest.

"No way," said Liam. "This place is technologically insanely advanced." So he sat down on the couch, to test the couches reaction.

"I would like a massage please." "Light or medium?" asked the couch. "I'll have a medium massage."

Two hands extended from the couch, and began massaging Liam's shoulders.

"This feels so good," he said.

Gladess now walked in with a notebook in her hand. "I see you are getting quite comfortable." "I have addressed the issue of your sister accompanying you, your name is girl?"

"My name is Floza."

"So Mr. Hendo was kind enough to agree to see both off you."

"Right this way, he is ready for you both."

It was time to meet Mr. Hendo Wallens. Floza had felt very nervous, even more nervous than Liam. She had never met Mr. Hendo in person, accept for seeing him in the newspaper.

"Are you ready Liam," she asked.

"I don't think I will ever be ready Floza."

"We shall try our best, and Floza if something happens to me, please take the news to my father."

"What do you mean Liam?" nothing is going to happen.

"No Floza, just promise me, if something happens, you will give the news to my father."

"Promise me Floza" with not much of a choice Floza promised Liam.

"I'm waiting," said Gladess.

"Mr. Hendo does not have all day you know, he is a very busy man." "Mr. Hendo's office is on the very last floor."

"What floor number would that be?" asked Floza.

"Floor number ninety-nine," replied Gladess.

"That is a long way up," said Liam.

"Hendo Enterprises is the tallest building in the world. Mr. Hendo designed the building himself; you may be able to see a few clouds on your way up. Don't be too alarmed," replied Gladess.

The elevator stopped at floor ninety-nine.

"Come along," said Gladess. Gladess walked out of the elevator, and Liam and Floza followed. As they walked, they noticed clouds outside; they covered the building like thick fog.

"There is not much light in here, because of the clouds," said Gladess. "This is Mr. Hendo's office, wait here while I check if he is ready." So Gladess went into Mr. Hendo's office, and she walked out very quickly.

"He is ready for you," she said.

Liam opened the door, for Floza to walk through first. There seemed to be no one in the room. There was music in the background, it sounded like the opera. There was a big chair behind a desk; it was faced the other way, and suddenly it turned. There was a man sitting in this chair. He was thin and pale, he wore a green suit with a bow tie, and on his head was a top hat. This man had a peculiar smile; it was sort of creepy like that of a clown. This man was Mr. Hendo Wallens, the most powerful man in Durbey.

"Pleased to meet you Mr. Hendo Wa...wallens," said Liam. He was rather nervous being in the presence of the most powerful man in Durbey.

"Liam and Floza, I am Mr. Hendo Wallens. Welcome to my enterprise, not many have seen inside the walls of Hendo Enterprises. You must consider yourselves very lucky," said Mr. Wallens.

"Are you sure you both are related?" asked Mr. Wallens.

"Yes, we are, why do you ask?" replied Floza.

"Well you don't look the same, not one bit actually. Never mind that, why have you come to see me boy?" asked Mr. Wallens.

"What was so important that you had to speak to me in person. I have thousands of employees here at Hendo Enterprises, so I asked Gladess why I should meet with this boy specifically. She mentioned something about your father, an employee of Hendo Enterprises is he?" asked Mr. Hendo as he grinned from ear to ear.

He jumped of his seat and walked to what looked like a portrait of himself. He stood there mimicking the pose in the portrait.

"Why is he doing that?" asked Floza.

"I don't know," replied Liam. "He seems to be all over the place. Mr. Hendo, my father is an employee of Hendo Enterprises. He is unfortunately in no state to return to work, hence my visit this morning."

"No state, no state you say.... I was never really in a state to be this powerful but I made myself this way. Your father will return to work, he is bound here," said Mr. Hendo.

"Mr. Hendo, my father is not well enough to work; if he comes back to Hendo Enterprises he will die," said Liam.

"Die! Oh no, he will die!" replied Mr. Hendo, placing his fingers on his mouth. He seemed very condescending, he was not taking Liam seriously either.

"Did you know that my employees are bound to me, to Hendo Enterprises, till death do we part?" he said with a smug look on his face.

"Yes, I do Mr. Hendo," said Liam.

"So, you do know?" asked Mr. Hendo. "Yes," replied Liam.

"So... why have you come here boy? Did you think, I was going to do you a favor? Did you think I was going to release your father from his duties? Oh no...... this is the first time you have met Mr. Hendo Wallens. Many of my employees pass on, it is a part of their commitment to the enterprise."

"How else would Durbey be such a well-established City, without sacrifice? They have died for a good cause, and will continue to do so," said Mr. Hendo without a slight feeling of remorse.

"Please Mr. Hendo, there must be a way, my father is the only family I have please release him from the magical contract," begged Liam.

"You mean this magical contract?" Mr. Hendo had made Mr. Luke's contract of employment appear in thin air; he cast it up and down and played with it like it was a useless piece of paper.

"This is your fathers contract, you see he signed his name right here."

Mr. Hendo had now shown Liam and Floza Mr. Luke's signature on the magical contract. He then began reading

I Mr. Luke, solemnly swear to be bound
to Hendo Enterprises for life.

"The clause clearly states boy, once the person places his signature on the contract, he or she will be bound for life - to me," and the contract then vanished.

"You see boy, I cannot help you, no employee has left Hendo Enterprises without falling to the ground. For those who have attempted to will not go very far either," he said as looked at Floza.

"There is no escaping me, Mr. Hendo Wallens," he said as he shook his head with excitement.

"Now off with you, I have so many important things to do."

"I am not leaving," said Liam, "You have to help me." "I don't have to do anything boy, your weak father belongs to me, so see to it that he returns to Hendo Enterprises or I will send my men to fetch him," said Hendo Wallens.

"I have come with a request," said Liam in a loud voice.

"Request? Are you requesting from me?" asked Mr. Hendo.

"Yes, I am requesting that you release my father, and I will work in his place. I will sign the magical contract, I will be bound to you and Hendo Enterprises for life, if you grant me this request," said Liam.

"Hmm, fresh blood, young and energetic I presume. I have never granted such requests, well no one has ever requested this before. Are you willing to sacrifice your life for your father, boy?" asked Mr. Hendo.

"No, no he cannot!" yelled Floza.

"Floza! Stop this, I told you not to speak!" said Liam. "Wow is there love here?" asked Mr. Hendo.

"I am willing to sacrifice my life, I will replace my father from now on," said Liam.

"Good, then you will sign the magical contract," said Mr. Hendo, and a new contract with Liam's name appeared on the table.

"Please Mr. Hendo, don't take Liam. Let his father go as well. It is the right thing to do," begged Floza.

"I won't," said Mr. Hendo, "because I can do whatever I want, the people of Durbey owe me. They were nothing before I came to Durbey, very much like that lousy place you come from, Clobet Valley."

"What! I don't know what you are talking about," gulped Floza.

She could not believe that Mr. Hendo had known that she was in fact from Clobet Valley, but how could he know? Unless… Edor had told him this, but then where is Edor now? Could it be that Edor works for Mr. Hendo?"

"Floza enough," said Liam.

"I am ready to sign the contract, so he took the pen from the table and signed the contract. Once he had completed the contract its color changed to gold."

"It's now sealed and binding," smiled Mr. Hendo. "What about my father's contract?" asked Liam. "You mean this?" and Mr. Hendo made Mr. Luke's contract magically appear once again. It hovered in the air. It seemed as if these contracts were controlled by the magic of Mr. Hendo.

"I break the bond between Mr. Luke and Hendo Enterprises, he is released," said Mr. Hendo and the contract burned until it was reduced to ash.

"There now, come along, you have work to do."

"You mean Liam is going to start work immediately?" asked Floza.

"He will do as I say, he now belongs to me… and I order that he starts working immediately," said Mr. Hendo.

"Mr. Hendo, I would like to see my father one last time… please Sir," begged Liam.

"Don't be ridiculous, you no longer have family, do not speak of the outside world, or if you do the punishment will be severe," said Mr. Hendo his eyes growing larger.

"Floza please do what I asked of you," said Liam as he lowered his head. "I now belong to you, Mr. Hendo."

"That sounds more like it," replied Mr. Hendo, delighted about his new recruit.

"So, Miss Floza, is it not time for you to leave?" asked Mr. Hendo.

"Actually, I don't want to leave just yet. Erm, I would like to speak to Liam in person," replied Floza.

"Not possible! That cannot happen," retorted Mr. Hendo.

"Why not? It's just to say goodbye," replied Floza. "Because I don't feel like it," he said.

"No, please Mr. Hendo, I beg you," said Floza. "Guards", he said and within a minute two Conploys walked into the office.

"Escort this girl out," ordered Mr. Hendo. "Yes Mr. Hendo Sir," replied the Conploys.

So the guards grabbed Floza and pulled her out of the room, she shuffled and kicked as to resist them. But they were too strong for her.

"There was no need for you to do that, Mr. Hendo," said Liam in an angry tone.

"Oops, how silly of me, did I just kick out the women you care about?" Mr. Hendo said laughing.

"Floza and I are just friends," said Liam.

"So you're not family? But I knew this already," sneered Mr. Hendo.

"How could you possibly know this?" asked Liam.

"I know everything, everything about your friend Floza," said Mr. Hendo with a big smile on his face.

"What could you possibly know about Floza?" questioned Liam.

"Oh…. never mind what I know about her," replied Mr. Hendo. "Now come along boy, it's time for you to start working. Gladess! Call for Mugbie at once, I have a new addition to his workforce, an energetic young man," said Mr. Hendo while speaking over the phone.

"Knock, knock." There was someone at the door. "Come in Mugbie."

"Sir you called for me?" asked Mugbie.

"Yes! This boy has just signed a contract with Hendo Enterprises. He is so.... eager to start work. See to it that he gets a pair of overalls and a number too."

"Yes Sir, replied Mugbie while bowing his head. "Come along boy," shouted Mugbie.

"My name is Liam, Sir."

"You don't have a name anymore, from now on you will be called by your number," said Mugbie with a large grin on his face.

Liam was then taken to join the other employees of Hendo Enterprises. He was now just a number; his life was doomed. There was no way that he could escape the situation he was in, he now belonged to Mr. Hendo Wallens.

Meanwhile Floza was escorted out of Hendo Enterprises, it was the first time she was treated like a prisoner, and this made her feel furious at Mr. Hendo. For taking Liam as his employee, and the manner in which he ordered she leave the enterprise.

"Let me go, get your hands of me," said Floza.

The Conploys escorted her through a long hallway. As she was escorted, she kicked and shuffled for the guards to release her.

"Relax girl, we are just doing our job," they said. "Your job! You are just an experiment of Mr. Hendo, he is just using you for your nine lives," shouted Floza. "We already know this girl," said one of the Conploys,

"We don't have a choice, we belong to him."

Something in the Hallway caught Floza's eye; it was a picture frame on the wall.

"Wait!" she said, "Who is this in the picture? This panther, what is he doing here?" asked Floza.

On the walls of the hallway were many picture frames of Mr. Hendo, but one stood out. It was in fact a picture of a black panther that looked like Edor. He was sitting on the very same chair Mr. Hendo sat on, and in the very same location.

"The panther? Are you serious girl?" asked the Conploy.

"The panther in the picture is Mr. Hendo Wallens himself. Were you not aware that he is in fact also a panther?"

Floza looked at the picture frame stunned. "Mr. Hendo is a panther," she repeated.

"Yes. He has the ability to transform into a black panther, in fact any animal he wishes to transform into," explained the Conploy. "His panther name is ...."

"Edor," finished Floza, completing the sentence of the Conploy.

"Yes... so you do know, Mr. Hendo Edor Wallens is his name."

"Well you learn something new every day, don't you?" replied Floza.

"I can't believe this Edor is Mr. Hendo Wallens, the most powerful man in Durbey. This is so confusing, I trusted Edor, he convinced me to come to Durbey," thought Floza.

"He said he had the cure for my father that I had to come with him to his world. When all this time he was none other than Mr. Hendo Wallens, the most powerful man in Durbey. It makes much more sense now. The Conploy said that Mr. Hendo has the ability to transform into any animal. Mr. Hendo was actually Popsicle, at least for some time he posed as Mrs. Poppsy's pet. It was only before my father became ill that he presented himself as Edor, until he convinced me to come to Durbey."

"That's enough," said the Conploy, "You need to leave Hendo Enterprises."

So they pulled Floza away from the hall and took her to the entrance of Hendo Enterprises. They left her at the gateway and ordered she leave immediately.

"Open the gates," shouted one Conploy. So the gates opened. One of the Conploys pushed Floza forward, to get her move. Floza walked out of the gates of Hendo Enterprises.

She stopped for a moment and looked back at the massive building that stood before her. Everything that had happened today felt like a bad dream, a series of unexpected events.

Her dear friend Liam was now at the mercy of Mr. Hendo. After seeing the picture of Edor, she had accidently found out that he was in fact Mr. Hendo himself. It was a total mystery, as to why Edor had lured her to Durbey. There were so many unanswered questions in Floza's mind.

"Why did Edor choose me? Is there really a cure? How do I get back home?"

The young girl who had been on a mission to save her father now felt betrayed. It was Edor who she had trusted to produce the cure. Now she was all alone in a strange city with no clue of what was to come next.

Floza made her way back to Eva's women's home. As she walked her head remained down.

"Why so down?" asked Gracy, as Floza walked through the entrance. Floza remained absolutely silent, she did not feel like speaking. The lady cats were still at work, the hostel was rather quiet. Since she had no one to talk to, Floza decided to lie in bed for a while. She laid there sobbing thinking of how her disappearance would have worried her father. She also thought about her father's condition and wondered whether he was doing well. Since there was no way she was going to get the cure from Edor, the only action Floza could now take was to return to Clobet Valley.

"It was all a lie," she thought.

"What do I do now? I have to leave this place, I have to go back to Clobet Valley. But how? Edor would never take me back home. My only chance of returning home is if I win the Durbey Talent show. I will use the teleporting bubble to go back home, that is if I win first place.

Everyone in Durbey would need to vote me the best performer. I have to practice immediately; if I don't win the show, I will be stuck in Durbey forever. It's time to start practicing, I cannot afford to lose. My life depends on it!"

Floza now began to rehearse her item for the talent show, she used the radio and a mix-tape which Stacy had made for her. The music on the mix-tape was very modern, it was quite difficult to compose a dance item using this type of music. Since Floza had never been exposed to electro beat music, it was very fast, but the ballet mix tamed it down a bit.

"How will I dance to this? I'm required to move quite fast." thought Floza. "Unless I add in a few hand stands? I'm quite good at those."

So Floza decided to try something different, she did really well for her first time dancing to this type of music. She tried all sorts of things, jumping, waving her hands. Some actually looked quite strange, but her body was in rhythm with the music.

This dance routine revealed a different side to Floza's character, some hidden talent that she had never known existed. It was nothing like the dancing her father wanted her to perfect, she definitely was not a swan, but rather she looked more like a funky canary on the dance floor. The most important part of this was that she felt the happiest she had felt for a very long time.

'Only one more sleep till the Durbey Talent show' stated the headlines of the Durbey News Paper. Stacy had walked in with the newspaper in her hands; she read it aloud to Floza.

"So, I see you are practicing," said Stacy. "Can you perhaps, start from the beginning, so I can tell you what I think?"

"One more sleep…. we don't have enough time left," exclaimed Floza.

"I need to see your whole dance item first, I'll pretend to be one of the judges this time," replied Stacy.

So Floza put the mix-tape on the radio once again, and she started her dance item. This was the first time Stacy had seen her perform the whole dance in one go. As she was always busy at work, she did not have enough time to coach Floza.

"This is fantastic," said Stacy jumping up and down. "It is one of the best dance performances I have seen in a very long time. You have nothing to fear my friend, you are well prepared for tomorrow night."

"Are you sure?" asked Floza.

It was a time of mixed emotions and feelings for Floza; on the one hand she was worried about Liam, and on the other she was excited to be participating in one of the biggest events in Durbey. Since her dear friend Liam was now bound to Hendo Enterprises, she was not going to engage with him in a very long time.

He was now the property of Mr. Hendo, a mere robot, just like Stacy. Deep inside Floza's heart she wished that the teleporting bubble could be hers. She had no intention of using the device for the wrong reasons. It was purely her love and devotion to her father Loops that made her aspire to be the winner of the Durbey Talent Show. It was a challenging task, to be selected as the number one top performer in the whole of Durbey.

"Stacy…. can you tell me a bit more about what to expect at the Durbey Talent Show?" she asked.

"Let me see what it says in the paper," replied Stacy and she went on to read more about the most famous event in Durbey.

"It says in the Durbey News Paper that the show is to be judged by the three most famous people in Durbey, namely Rock Cukooo who is a famous artist and singer."

"Rock Cukooo," replied Floza.

"Yes, he is one of the most famous artists, a composer of digital rock music," explained Stacy.

"The second judge elected by the Durbey Talent Committee was the alluring Selva Pop, also known as Pin Pop who was a multi-awarding winning pop star and brand ambassador for the motorized skates on wheels."

"Skates on Wheels, whatever is that?" asked Floza. "Skates on wheels are very much like roller skates, it is a common hobby enjoyed by many of the people of Durbey," replied Stacy. "It is very much like shoes with wheels, the only difference with the motorized skates is that you do not have to do much leg work, the motor moves the skates for you."

"Why would anyone want shoes with wheels on them?" thought Floza.

"We are also pleased to announce the third judge at the Durbey Talent show," read Stacy as she smiled. "His first public appearance in five years, the richest and most powerful man in Durbey, none other than Mr. Hendo Wallens.

Floza, I cannot believe what I have just read. Look at this, it says in the newspaper that Mr. Hendo is going to be a judge in the talent show."

Floza quickly pulled the newspaper from Stacy's hand, and looked at the latest article on the Durbey Fair. She starred hard for a while until she found the piece on the Durbey Talent Show.

"Whaaaattt!!!! Who elected him to be a judge at the show?" she said.

"He must have bought his way in, after all what does he know about talent?"

"Mr. Hendo is the sponsor of the grand prize Floza, I don't think he needs a special invitation since he is the most powerful man in Durbey," replied Stacy.

"You are right Stacy, he himself wants to select the best person for his precious teleporting bubble," replied Floza as she squashed the newspaper with frustration.

"I can never win now, he definitely remembers me accompanying Liam to Hendo Enterprises, he will never let me win," she thought.

"What are you so angry about?" asked Stacy.

"I... accompanied Liam to Enterprises, I was going to tell you," admitted Floza.

"What for? Why would Liam want to go to Hendo Enterprises?" asked Stacy.

"Well Stacy... we went to meet Mr. Hendo, Liam had a proposal for him, he wanted to free his father from the magical contract, and so I decided to accompany him," answered Floza.

"Are you telling me, that you have seen Mr. Hendo, face to face?" asked Stacy.

"Yes, we did, until.... Liam was taken away," cried Floza. I tried to stand up to Mr. Hendo.

"Stood up?" asked Stacy.

"Yes, I told Mr. Hendo that he is just horrible, and what he is doing to people is just wrong. He ordered his guards to escort me out of Hendo Enterprises, I did not get a chance to say goodbye to Liam. Now... Edor remembers me, he will never let me win the Durbey Talent Show," replied Floza.

"Edor remembers you? Did you see Mr. Hendo transform into a black panther Floza?" asked Stacy.

"No...but as the guards escorted me through the hall way, I saw a picture on the wall, it was a black panther. A panther I have met before," replied Floza.

"You mean, you saw a picture of Mr. Hendo in his cat form?" asked Stacy.

"Yes, I had no idea that Mr. Hendo was in fact Mr. Hendo Edor Wallens," said Floza.

"Everyone in Durbey knows about Edor. I presumed you would have known as well," said Stacy.

"I guess I could not have known, since I am not from Durbey," replied Floza.

"You mean you lied to me?" asked Stacy.

"When all this time I felt guilty that I had not told you that I was in fact a Conploy."

"I am sorry Stacy, I did lie," said Floza as she lowered her head down in disappointment.

"I could not mention to anyone that I was not from Durbey. I promised Edor that I would keep this a secret."

"Well if you are not from Durbey, where are you from?" asked Stacy.

"Clobet Valley," replied Floza.

"Clobet Valley..." repeated Stacy, "I have not heard of this place before."

"It is a place unknown to many, a beautiful little village on the border of a valley," explained Floza. "This valley was discovered by my father and his friends, I have lived there ever since I was a baby, the people are so kind and we live in harmony."

"Then why would you leave your home to come to this horrid place?" asked Stacy.

"I don't think Durbey is horrid, it is a beautiful city, with so much splendor, however this thing called money is making some happy, and for those who don't have it, their lives are a nightmare," replied Floza.

"It was not my choice to come to Durbey, in fact at the time I did not have an option. You see Stacy, my father fell ill, with a virus. Our doctor could not find a cure in time, so Edor approached me; he told me to come to Durbey, where he would present me with the cure."

"What.... Edor was at Clobet Valley?" asked Stacy.

"Yes, he posed as Popsicle for a while, a little Persian cat who lived with our friend, until one night he transformed and visited me with his proposal," explained Floza.

"What about your father? I mean you have been away from Clobet Valley for more than a month now, and he still does not have a cure."

"The funny thing is that Edor gave me a temporary cure before we left, he said that it would sustain my father's health, until we had come to Durbey," said Floza.

"I am not trying to frighten you Flo, but do you really believe that Edor would actually save a person?" asked Stacy.

"After finding out the truth, that Edor is in fact Mr. Hendo, I don't believe that he wanted to save my father. But I will have to find out the reason he lured me to Durbey. I will need to go back to Clobet Valley, and the only way back home is with the teleporting bubble."

Floza now felt that her chances of winning the teleporting bubble were very slim, since Mr. Hendo would remember the little commotion she had caused at Hendo Enterprises."

"Now... now Floza, don't cry. What if there was another way?" said Stacy.

"Another way?" asked Floza, wiping her tears.

"Yes...what if we made you look so different that he would not even recognize you?" said Stacy.

"Like a disguise?" asked Floza.

"Well not entirely a disguise, but sort of a costume with a mask, in that way he would not recognize your face."

"What about my name? He will definitely recognize that!" said Floza.

"Well, maybe you could change your name," replied Stacy trying to think of a solution.

"You mean lie about my name?" asked Floza.

"No don't be silly, I don't mean that, you can call yourself something different, like a stage name," said Stacy.

"Stage name…." replied Floza. "I wonder what a stage name could be. How about 'the ballerina'?"

"Err, that's too cheesy," replied Stacy, "It has to be captivating, something like 'The Dancer'!"

"How about… the 'Durbey Dancer'?" asked Floza.

"Yes! You've got it, I love the sound of that!" shouted Stacy.

"Floza… the 'Durbey Dancer'!!"

"Stacy, now the 'Durbey Dancer' needs to go to bed, she has a big day ahead of her," said Floza.

"Sure…" yawned Stacy, you will do so well tomorrow night, I believe in you."

Floza walked forward to Stacy and hugged her, she felt so much comfort. Stacy was such a good friend, she always made her smile, even though this was one of the most difficult times in her life.

"I have a masquerade mask that you may use as a disguise," said Stacy.

"Excellent!!" replied Floza, "I can't wait to see what it looks like! This mask is going to look terrific with my costume."

"Costume?" repeated Stacy, looking confused.

"Come along Stacy, I have a surprise," said Floza.

They both walked together to the bedroom, she opened the closet and took out the bag in which her costume was.

"Close your eyes Stacy….".

Floza took out the costume from the bag, and held it up for Stacy to see.

"You may open your eyes now," she said, and so Stacy did.

"Oh, my goodness, said Stacy. This is absolutely beautiful, it's dazzling."

"I got it from a store called Bedazzle, and at a good price too," replied Floza.

"It's perfect, you certainly will be noticed tomorrow night. This makes me feel even more excited."

So Floza tried on her costume once again, together with the masquerade mask Stacy had given to her. With only one more sleep to the Durbey Talent show, both the girls were excited and nervous at the same time.

CHAPTER 13

CLOBET FAIR

It was the time of year again when the people of Clobet Valley prepared for the annual fair. Mrs. Poppsy was rather busy getting the pets ready for the 'Posh pets competition'. She thought so much of Popsicle during this time.

He was always a contestant in the competition, and a three-time first prize winner. It was two weeks since the elders had last met, and during this time there had been no idea of where Floza could be. The elders had decided to meet at the barnyard, which was one of the venues for the Clobet fair.

It was at this very meeting that the elders would present their evidence, and so Mrs. Poppsy drew a sketch of the strange man as Loops had requested. Loops had brought Rods with him since it was raining and he did not like being alone when it rained.

"Evening friends, it is good to see you. I thought that it was about time we bring forward our evidence," said Loops.

"Indeed, I think we have all had sufficient time to gather our evidence," replied Headmaster Nimble.

"Now who shall present first?"

The elders looked around the table, waiting for a reaction.

"I'll go first," said Mrs. Poppsy.

"Together with Nimble, we would like to present our information obtained from the guards at the borders."

"Go ahead," replied Loops.

"So, the information that Nimble and I obtained may not be well understood, we are both still curious as to what the guards meant. The guards reported that there was no sighting of any foreign individual. They also went on to say that, they have been on duty quite diligently. The only thing that stood out for them, which they felt was strange, was a sighting of a foreign object in the sky. This was approximately the same morning Floza disappeared," said Mrs. Poppsy.

"The guards also reported that the strange object was seen again the day the strange man visited us all," added Headmaster Nimble.

"Strange object?" asked Dr. Hoppins.

"Did the guards provide any details about this flying object?" asked Loops.

"The only thing mentioned," said Mr. Nimble, "Was that it looked like a floating bubble, but what was strange is that there seemed to be a person inside."

"So... how about the morning Floza went missing?" asked Loops.

"Yes, the floating object was identified, but it was too far away to see who was inside," replied Mrs. Poppsy.

"Anything else you both would like to share?" asked Loops.

"No that will be all," replied Mrs. Poppsy.

"I will present my findings," replied Loops.

"My findings on this," said Loops. He took out a small pill from his pocket. It was the same pill that had been given to him the night Edor had visited Floza.

"What about this pill?" asked Dr. Hoppins.

"This is the very same pill that Floza gave to me, the pill that she said had come from you," replied Loops.

Dr. Hoppins took the pill from Loops to inspect it. "This surely, is not one of my medicines, I can tell by the type of coating on the pill."

"Are you sure doctor?" asked Mr. Thimble.

"Yes! I am certain that this is not one of my medicines," replied Dr. Hoppins.

"Then were did it come from?" asked Mrs. Poppsy.

"I found this pill outside, in my yard, it was lying there on the ground, until Rods showed me something close by. It was this."

Loops picked up the little box from the table and presented it to the friends.

"This is a medicine box," replied Headmaster Nimble.

"Yes, it is a medicine box, I presume it came from the person that handed over the pills to Floza," said Loops.

"It looks like it has some writing on it. Read it out would you?" said Mrs. Poppsy.

"On it is written IV258," replied Loops.

"IV258, that is a drug used to treat certain illness in cats," said Doctor Hoppins

"Cats!! Are you serious?"

"Why on earth would someone give Loops a pill that is used for cats," yelled Mrs. Poppsy.

"It was meant to debilitate him, to a point that would make him feel like he is dying," replied Dr. Hoppins.

"The drug is meant for animals yes, and if consumed by a human it would have an adverse effect on one's health such as fever, nausea and even hallucinations."

"Hence, I felt the fever and extremely painful headache," replied Loops.

"But who would do this to me? It just does not make sense. How is it that I regained my health after I was given a cure by Floza?"

"My understanding of this is that you were deliberately given the IV258 drug to make you ill, until you were presented with a cure, which would assist you to regain your health after a day," replied Dr. Hoppins.

"The very same drug that I am holding in my hand, friends. I presume it is a very strong antibiotic, it was meant to clear your body of the effects of IV258 Loops," continued Doctor Hoppins.

"All this was planned, well planned in fact. Now for me to present my evidence about the strange man. After speaking to Suzy, I found out who the strange man really was. The man who made his way to Clobet Valley, in a flying bubble, the man I presume took Floza and Popsicle. Suzy met this man the day Mrs. Poppsy directed him to my surgery; she described him as you did Mrs. Poppsy. He wore a long coat and a hat that covered his face."

"Then why did he not see you?" asked Headmaster Nimble.

"Apparently, he did intend to see me, but we had many patients waiting in line, and he had to leave. He then booked an appointment for the next day... but obviously he was gone by then and did not show up."

"He booked an appointment; did you perhaps ask Suzy under which name this man booked his appointment?" asked

Loops. All the elders were in suspense, all the evidence presented was leading to the strange man, but who was he?

"Yes Suzy did tell me, the name this man called himself…"

"And what was it?" asked Mrs. Poppsy, as the suspense was building up and all could not wait to hear who the strange man was.

"He told her that his name was Mr. Wallens!"

There was complete silence in the room after hearing the name Mr. Wallens. One could clearly see the sweat dripping from the faces of the elders, the flustered redness to their faces. Why were they so nervous on hearing the name Mr. Wallens? More importantly how did they know of Mr. Hendo Wallens?

"This is outrageous," said Headmaster Nimble as he woke up from his seat. "This is a lie! It can't be, there is no way that Hendo has found us, it's not possible. There is nothing that could have led him to us."

"Calm down, Nimble," said Dr, Hoppins. This is not a lie, it is a fact that all the evidence that has just been presented points to none other than Mr. Hendo Wallens."

"Yes, you are right, he is back," said Loops. "I suspected this from the time I saw the strange man, his voice sounded familiar and he looked like he was up to no good."

"This means that it was Mr. Hendo that took my dear Popsicle," said Mrs. Poppsy as she cried. "Yes indeed, it was Mr. Hendo that took my Floza, he was the one who gave her the cure. Perhaps he disguised himself like you Hoppins, to make Floza believe it was you that had given her the cure."

"It all makes sense now," replied Thimble. The information you wanted me to find out Loops, I would like to present now."

"Go ahead Thimble, tell us what you have found out."

"But we don't know what Thimble was going to investigate? You kept this between yourselves Loops," said Mrs. Poppsy. "What was so important that we could not hear for ourselves?"

"Mrs. Poppsy, The reason I kept this a secret with Thimble is to not scare you or our other friends, without getting the facts first, now please give Thimble a chance to speak."

"Indeed," replied Mrs. Poppsy.

"As I was saying, I was tasked to check whether what we brought to Clobet Valley is still safe," said Thimble.

"You mean the book?" asked Dr. Hoppins.

"Yes, Master Gillian's magic book, it seems it is safe, but for how long? Mr. Hendo has definitely found us, and the book will not be safe for too long. I went to the old cave, where the book was hidden all these years. I found that it was glowing so brightly that it lit the entire cave. This only means one thing; it has summoned the Master. Since Mr. Hendo has come to Clobet Valley, the book has started glowing, it is aware that its Master has returned."

"What do we do now?" asked Mrs. Poppsy. She was very frightened on hearing of the return of Mr. Hendo.

"We have to go back to Durbey. We will have to save Floza," replied Loops.

"Mr. Hendo wants his book back and I will take it to him, in exchange for my Floza."

"But you can't go. If you leave you may never come back," replied Dr. Hoppins.

"I will go with you," said Mr. Thimble. "So will I," said Headmaster Nimble.

"What about me?" replied Mrs. Poppsy, "I certainly cannot sit around and wait knowing that man has my Popsicle."

"Mrs. Poppsy, this might be too dangerous for you," replied Loops.

"We will take the book back to Durbey, and we will try our best to bring Popsicle home safely. But once we return the book to Mr. Hendo, what happens next? With access to all that magic, do you really believe that Mr. Hendo will spare us? We cannot only think about ourselves Loops," said Dr. Hoppins. "What about the people at Clobet Valley? Their lives are also in grave danger."

"Hoppins, what do you propose we do? What would you do if Suzy was taken by Mr. Hendo? Would you be content with her captured by Mr. Hendo?" said Loops. "You know very well how cruel he can be; he would not spare a fly, let alone our family members."

"I did not realize," said Dr. Hoppins. "To answer your question, I would save my granddaughter, since Mr. Hendo was the reason her mother had died. I could not bear to see Suzy go through the same fate as her mother."

Dr. Hoppins had lost his daughter, in a similar disappearance to Floza's. Suzy was a little baby when her mother had disappeared and Dr. Hoppins was left all alone to take care of his granddaughter.

"I ask myself, was it worth leaving Durbey behind, if we look at the damage it has caused our loved ones," replied Loops.

"If we only knew back then, I would have sacrificed my life for Hendo Enterprises, if it were to protect my family from Mr. Hendo Wallens. We have lost so much. I cannot lose Floza, I will not let that happen. We have to take the book back to him."

"You are right Loops," said Dr. Hoppins. "We were mere numbers of a contractual agreement made between him and ourselves. We belonged to him and our very lives were spent working for his cause, the only way to escape his tyranny was to leave Durbey. It was hard enough for me to raise a little girl on my own, due to the circumstances at Durbey. I still remember what it felt like to walk in the laboratories of the Hendo enterprises, and how proud I felt to be a part of something that seemed so meaningful at the time. His scrupulous ways of running the enterprise was seen as admirable by us all. But we failed, we failed to see that we were a part of his destructible plan of ruining the natural cause of existence."

"I think we need to move past this and I believe we will get Floza back very soon my dear friend Loops," said Mr. Thimble in a compassionate voice.

Mr. Thimble and Loops were particularly close, they both had worked quite closely together at Hendo Enterprises. The friends were responsible for conducting tests on different subjects in what was called the bypass room at Hendo Enterprises. Well, actually they did not have much of a choice at the time, it was customary that junior scientists work in the bypass room.

Their career started out in the order room, their main duties at the time were to collect and sort letters, these letters were mailed to Hendo Enterprises from people around the world. These people ordered all sorts of things from Hendo Enterprises, things related to new inventions, research and some fancied magic.

Now just to mention the magic I speak of is not just pulling rabbits from a hat. No, it was much more than mediocre magic tricks, voodoo and spells. The magic created at Hendo Enterprises was about creating illusions, changing the appearance of people and also the manipulation of time and space.

It was fascinating for a while, when the elders worked closely with Mr. Hendo, until experiments went wrong, people's lives were destroyed and in some instances, lives were lost. Mrs. Poppsy worked in the room of magical contracts, she was responsible for keeping all magical contracts locked away. Since this was a very important task that required much commitment, Mr. Hendo had brought in an outside woman who had no relations with other workers at Hendo

Enterprises. This woman was none other than Mrs. Poppsy; she was rather young at the time when she started out at Hendo Enterprises. As a young lady, Mrs. Poppsy was rather slim, she had just got married until her life changed for the worst. Since she started working for Mr. Hendo, she worked in isolation from the other workers. This was a requirement for her job, as keeper of magical contracts.

Things turned out very differently for Mrs. Poppsy when she met Loops and Thimble at Hendo Enterprises. It was when conditions got so bad at the Enterprise that the three would meet in secret to find ways to cope, until enough was enough.

Dr. Hoppins was a senior scientist at Hendo Laboratories; he was a doctor by profession but was employed at Hendo Enterprises, to conduct animal studies. It was at the very beginning of Dr. Hoppins career that Mr. Hendo requested that he conduct experiments on animals. He requested he experiment on mice until his desire for knowledge on other species began.

It was during this time that Mr. Hendo convinced Dr. Hoppins to work on his newly founded research, the composition of cat DNA. Dr. Hoppins could not question Mr. Hendo's orders and so proceeded with the research. Little did Dr. Hoppins know that his research would be the start of developing a new race of cat people, namely the Conploys. When Mr. Hendo discovered that cats' nine lives could be absorbed into human DNA, he was adamant that his creation of a new race of workers would change Hendo Enterprises and ultimately the world.

It was through the Cat DNA research that Dr. Hoppins formed a relationship with Headmaster Nimble, who was a laboratory worker at the time. Headmaster Nimble had a slightly more relaxed job compared to the other elders. Working in the laboratory had its advantages, it was away from the noise at Hendo Enterprises. Things were ordinary for Headmaster Nimble, until his mother fell ill, and being the only child, he was tasked to take care of his mother.

However, signing the magic contract had its limitations, Headmaster Nimble was not allowed to leave Hendo Enterprises because of the many projects he was supporting. He became desperate; he had to escape the imprisonment brought through the magical contract, and so the elders formed a union, and pledged together that one day they would leave Hendo Enterprises forever. That one day came very soon after. Mr. Hendo went on an expedition to Asia, and on his return, he had found that Hendo Enterprises had been destroyed and his magic book passed on by Master Gillian's had disappeared.

It was only after a count of all his employees that Mr. Hendo discovered that a few of his workers were missing, and those workers were none other than the elders of Clobet Valley.

"I still remember the day we escaped Hendo Enterprises," said Loops.

"Doctor, if it were not for your indestructible plan to acquire Master Gillian's book, we would never had made it to Clobet Valley."

"Oh nonsense, we all had a part to play in our escape," replied Doctor Hoppins.

"If it were not for Mrs. Poppsy's access to the magical contracts, we would never have broken the bond with Hendo Enterprises. Mr. Hendo thought that his magic was binding, and in essence it was, until we had the privilege of using Master Gillian's magic book to destroy our contracts."

"I agree, our story before Clobet Valley was indeed a complex one, but we fought through and we risked our very own lives, to create a free world for our friends and family," said Mr. Thimble.

Now that we have learnt that the elders of Clobet Valley were indeed workers of Hendo Enterprises, who were bonded by lifelong contracts, it is much clearer as to why, Edor or shall we call him Mr. Hendo Edor Wallens had secretly made his way to Clobet Valley. Mr. Hendo Edor Wallens now entered the lives of the elders once again, and now we understand that the elders of Clobet Valley were more than your ordinary and old-fashioned people who lived in a valley. Quite the contrary, they were quite the opposite with a mysterious and mystical background in each and every elder.

"What do we do now?" asked Mr. Thimble.

"We can only do one thing, we shall use the book to go back to Clobet Valley and we will rescue Floza and not forgetting Popsicle," replied Loops.

"What about the people of Clobet Valley, they are now in danger since we have exposed Mr. Hendo to our world?" asked Mrs. Poppsy with a concerned look on her face.

"I believe that there might be a spell of protection in Master Gillian's book, we will cast this over the valley before we leave, and the spell will ensure that no outside individuals can enter Clobet," replied Dr. Hoppins.

"That is a great idea," replied Headmaster Nimble.

"I suggest we go to the old cave tomorrow night. We shall then cast the spell of protection over Clobet, and since tomorrow is the Clobet Fair everyone will be too involved to notice the reaction from the spell," said Loops.

"But Loops, if we cast the spell of protection, there will surely be a reaction in the sky," replied Mrs. Poppsy. "Yes, I agree with Mrs. Poppsy, the barrier of protection will surely be seen by the people of Clobet," replied Headmaster Nimble.

"Then we shall announce to the people that we have prepared a special display for this year's Clobet Fair," said Loops.

"That could work, I will place my spotlights outside on the night of Clobet Fair, to make it more realistic," replied Dr. Hoppins.

"Doctor, that will surely make the spell look much more believable," replied Loops.

So the elders agreed to meet the night of Clobet Fair, to cast the spell of protection over the valley, and soon after they would embark on their trip to Durbey.

CHAPTER 14

THE DURBEY TALENT SHOW

It was the day of the Durbey Talent show and there was a buzz all around the City of Durbey. The Durbey fair had begun, and all the people of Durbey were so excited. It was a spectacular event that occupied the whole of Florence Gardens. There were roller coasters, all sorts of fun rides, magic and a number of fun activities during the day, and the highlight for the Durbey Fair was the Durbey Talent Show. Since the show was tonight, all the contestants were getting prepared for their big night, including Mr. Hendo.

"The big day is here Mugbie, have you got the teleporting bubble ready?" asked Mr. Hendo.

"Yes Mr. Hendo Sir," replied Mugbie as he walked in with the teleporting bubble. "Behold the teleporting bubble, the second bubble I have created especially for the Durbey Talent show."

"I can assure you Sir it is in working order, I tested it on a Comply, we sent him off to the North Pole, and he returned to Hendo Enterprises in perfect order," said Mugbie.

"That is magnificent, Mugbie," replied Mr. Hendo.

"The Conploy was lucky enough to return in one piece."
"Not so lucky for the first Conploy, we sent to the South Pole. He vanished and he is probably frozen to death as we speak," answered Mugbie.

"Well until his nine lives run out, he will definitely die," replied Mr. Hendo.

"Good work Mugbie! Now see to it that the bubble is escorted to the Durbey talent show on time."

"Yes Mr. Hendo Sir," replied Mugbie grinning as he walked out of the room.

Meanwhile at Eva's women's' hostel the lady cats were watching the Durbey Fair on the television. Since they could not turn back into their human form, they were not permitted to leave the hostel, many of them were sad about this, but it was strictly Mr. Hendo's orders that no Conploy attend the fair.

"Aww I wish I could go on the Ferris wheel," signed one of the lady cats as her ears lowered down.

"I wish we could all go to the Durbey Fair, look at all the fun those people are having. Floza will be participating in the biggest show in Durbey, I am feeling rather disappointed, that I cannot be there," replied Stacy.

"Now, now, there is nothing much you lady cats can do, after all Mr. Hendo will be there and if he sets his eye on you, all of you will be in big trouble," replied Floza.

"What if I disguised myself, I would hate to miss your performance," said Stacy.

"Well I would love for you to be there, but I would also be very sad if you were to get caught seen at the Durbey Fair, I have seen how Mr. Hendo reacts when he is angry, I would prefer you stay at the hostel and watch my performance on the television. You will still have a chance to vote for me, all you have to do is call into the Durbey voting booth," said Floza.

"At least I will have a chance to vote for you, I will make sure all the lady cats vote for you as well," replied Stacy.

"Actually, I am hoping that I will get many votes from the people of Durbey, I feel very nervous that Mr. Hendo is a judge at the talent show, he will have a big say in the final results," said Floza.

"Yes indeed. He will have a say, but if the majority of Durbey vote for you as the best performer, there is nothing much Mr. Hendo can do," stated Sara.

"It's time for you to get your beauty rest, since you have practiced so much, I am sure you are feeling exhausted," said Stacy.

"Good idea, taking a nap will do me some good, please make sure I wake up in time. I cannot afford to be late for my performance," said Floza.

"Don't stress about that, I will make sure you wake up in time for your big event," replied Stacy.

"Now go on, we only have a few hours till the big event."

So Floza went to bed, and the cat ladies continued to watch the live broadcast of the Durbey fair on the television. It was six o clock and only two hours to go to the Durbey Talent show. Stacy walked to the room, ready to wake Floza for her big night.

"Wake up, Floza," she yelled.

"You have only two hours, till the talent show."

"I did not realize, I slept that long, I must say I feel rather energized."

"I shall get out of bed, and get ready immediately."

All contestants needed to be at least an hour early at the show so Floza changed into her costume. She was then approached by Gracy who offered to do her make up. It was quite unexpected, but Gracy had heard from the other cat ladies that Floza was to take part in the Durbey Talent show, and she was quite excited.

"Floza, it would be good if you had a bit of make up with your costume," she said.

"Make up. Oh no, that is not needed, in fact I will be wearing a mask, I will not need to have my face done up," said Floza.

"Nonsense! I am sure we can add some color to your cheeks and gloss for your lips," replied Gracy.

"I agree Gracy, you may get started," replied Stacy not giving Floza much of a choice to refuse.

After Gracy had completed her makeup, Floza was now ready to go to the Durbey Fair. All the cat ladies were amazed how beautiful she looked.

"It's too bad you have to wear that mask of yours," said Stacy, "especially since Gracy has done such a good job with your make up."

"It's time I left; wish me luck Stacy," said Floza.

"Best of luck, I know you will do very well, and Floza, remember that although I cannot be physically there to cheer you on, I will be cheering you on from a distance," said Stacy.

"Oh Stacy, thank you for everything," said Floza and she reached out to hug her dear friend.

"Now you'd best be off, the teleporting bubble will be yours," replied Stacy in confidence.

"No Stacy, the teleporting bubble will be ours," said Floza.

Stacy smiled, she then closed the door to the women's hostel, and went back to join the other lady cats, who were watching the broadcast on the television.

Floza was now on her own; she walked down the street in the direction of Florence Gardens, she thought about how proud Loops would be, if he had known that she was to take part in the biggest event in Durbey. Tonight, was the most important time in her stay at Durbey, it was the night that would determine if she were to stay in Durbey forever, or win the teleporting bubble that would send her back home.

"The Durbey Fair... Wow! It looks spectacular, and much better in real life," she thought.

"Ticket Miss," asked the man at the entrance.

"I am actually a contestant in tonight's Talent Show," replied Floza as she smiled with excitement.

"I see, so that will be a free entry for you. I was asked to direct all contestants to the stage area," replied the man.

"Oh yes, I need to know where to go, I can't afford to get lost in this big place," said Floza.

"Do you see, the lights beaming out into the sky?" asked the man.

"Uhhhh, yes I do," replied Floza.

"That is where the stage is, and you may now enter the Durbey Fair," said the man.

Floza could not believe that she was actually walking in Florence Gardens, the garden was transformed so well for the Durbey Fair. There were hundreds of people at the fair, all smiles, enjoying the rides and entertainment. The trees were covered in magnificent lights, with so many rides to choose from.

The ride that stood out the most was the rollercoaster. It covered the entire park, as it moved with accelerating speed, its electric colors lit up the sky.

"So, this is the Durbey Fair, it's so spectacular," thought Floza. "Father and Rods would be so excited to see this. I am getting much closer… to the beaming light. I must be close to the stage."

"Look dad, a beautiful ballerina," said a little girl pointing to Floza.

Floza picked up her hand to wave at the little girl, she was glad that she was noticed.

"Finally, I have reached the stage," said Floza as her eyes lit up.

She was amazed how big the stage was; it was lit up with many colors and surrounding the area were many people with cameras. To the front of the stage was a long table with a few chairs, for the judges to be seated.

"I assume you are here to take part in the Durbey Talent Show," asked a posh lady.

"Yes Miss, I am here as a contestant," replied Floza. "Good. You may join the other contestants back stage," said the lady as she stared at Floza in a peculiar manner.

Backstage was absolute chaos. The workers were franticly walking about, checking if all was in order for the show. Some of the contestants were already there, make-up artists and hair stylists were working on their appearance as they sat behind big mirrors.

It seemed like many of the contestants were doing different acts, some carried instruments, others wore outstanding costumes. It felt tense for a moment as Floza walked into the change area; there was a vibe of competitiveness, she could sense this when other contestants starred at her.

"No mother, this is not what I want to look like," yelled a young girl.

She was one of the contestants, and it was clear that she was rather spoilt. Her blonde hair was tied up with a ribbon, and she wore an alluring pink dress. Her pretty face was done up perfectly and in her hand, she carried a flute.

"Dear… you look absolutely gorgeous," replied the lady who seemed to be her mother. She looked rather flustered trying to convince her spoilt daughter that she in fact did look good.

"But mother, this is not the dress I ordered!" shouted the girl while placing her arms to the side.

"The show is about to start!" shouted one of the backstage workers.

"All contestants wait in line."

All the contestants now moved closely together, until a lady walked in with a pack of cards in her hand.

"These are numbers," she said, and she handed them out to all the contestants.

"When we call your number, you may then come forward, and enter the stage."

"Please do so in an orderly fashion," said the backstage worker.

"Number ten," read Floza. It seemed she had to wait for nine performances. It was quite a wait, and enough time for nerves to build up.

"Please see to it that you hand in your audio before your performance," said the backstage worker to all the contestants.

"Audio, what is that?" thought Floza.

"Excuse me, what is this audio that the lady speaks of?" asked Floza to a boy who was also one of the contestants. He seemed to be wearing a black cape and a top hat, he was going to be doing a magic performance.

"She means music," replied the boy.

"Oh yes, she means the music I will dance to. Let's see."

Floza reached inside her little bag, she shuffled around trying to get hold of the disc which Stacy had made especially for the contest. But there was nothing, she found the gloss and the ticket, but there was no music disc.

"Oh my goodness, could it be that I left the disc back at the hostel?" thought Floza.

"I am so stupid! What do I do now?" she said, as she burst in to tears.

"I will never make it back in time if I get the tape from Eva's hostel. I am ruined, I will be stuck in Durbey forever, I will never see father or Rods again, father will never know the reason as to why I left him."

It was a moment of complete sadness for Floza. Her only hope of travelling back home, was now ruined and it was all her own fault. She kneeled down on the floor and as she cried, the makeup Gracy had applied trickled down her face.

"Attention contestants. There is an announcement, we have an old lady looking for a Miss Floza, she has brought something for her," said a voice.

"That's me," replied Floza. "But who could this old lady be?"

"Miss, I am Floza, you mentioned that an old lady was here for me?" asked Floza.

"Yes, come this way. Please make this quick, non-contestants are not allowed back stage."

The worker escorted Floza to meet the old lady, and as they walked, she noticed there was indeed a person waiting for her. This person's face was covered with a scarf. It looked like an old lady hunched over with a walking stick.

"Can you give me a minute alone," said Floza.

"Sure," replied the backstage worker.

"You have come to see me. Who are you?" asked Floza.

"I am your grandmother," replied the old lady in a strange tone.

"Grandmother? But I don't have a grandmother," said Floza.

"I have come to give you this," said the old lady, reaching out her hand and placing a disc in Floza's hand.

The old lady's hands felt quite rough, and when Floza looked closely she noticed that it was in fact covered with fur.

"Pssst it's me, Stacy, said the lady, I disguised myself, I found the disc in the radio, just before you left the hostel. I knew that you would be panicking, so I decided to disguise myself with the help of the other cat ladies, and we came up with this look."

"What do you think of my performance?" asked Stacy. "Stacy is that you?" replied Floza. "Is this for real, have you brought me the music disc?"

"Yes. it's me Floza, now take it and I wish you luck once again. I'd best be off now, I can't afford to let anyone see me." So, Stacy hurried off before she could be noticed.

"Stacy what would I do without you?" smiled Floza. How relieved she felt, that's what friends are for, and Stacy was indeed a good friend, she was always looking out for Floza. It was now time for the show to start; all the contestants felt so nervous. The show was presented by a famous celebrity, television personality Hip Lee Louw. Hip Lee wore a silvery suit, and shades to match, and his energetic personality made the show much more exciting.

"Welcome Durbey to the 20th Annual Talent Show. We have three amazing guests this evening, who will judge the winner for tonight. Please put your hands together for the best electric music performer, rock and roller, Rock Cuckoo," said the presenter.

Rock cuckoo was a funky dressed rock star, he was a famous artist known by all in Durbey. The crowd went wild on his entrance, and he waved his arms up and around to make his presence known.

"Be prepared for our next guest to roll her way in, the brand ambassador of the motorized skates on wheels, multi-award-winning artist also known as Pin Pop, please put your hands together for Selva Pin Pop!" said the presenter.

Pin Pop entered the crowd in absolute style, she wore her famous brand motorized skates, she made her entrance on her motorized skates on wheels. The crowd was astonished, some fainted and others could not help screaming her name Pin Pop.

Hip Lee showed her to the judges booth, and so she took her seat. There was now only one guest to appear before the crowd.

"Citizens of Durbey, it's been five years since his public appearance, the man we owe everything too, the man who has made Durbey the most spectacular place to live in, he is the richest and most powerful, the master of magic, greatest scientist of the world. Please everyone stands up and applauds, Mr. Hendo Edor Wallens!!!!"

The crowd was ecstatic; some were sweating, others crying, it was as if the creator of the world had come before their very eyes. There was a drum roll for the special guest, smoke was in the air, until Mr. Hendo appeared to the crowds of people. He made a grand entrance, he flew in with what looked like a flying hoverboard. Mr. Hendo flew over the crowd, dressed in his green suit with a top hat on his head. He waved to the crowds of people. He had a huge smile on his face, like that of a clown, a sort of creepy smile. The people of Durbey were stunned to see Mr. Hendo Wallens before them; they stood up and clapped continuously until the hoverboard landed. Hip Lee was also stunned to be in the presence of Mr. Hendo Wallens himself, and directed him to the judges booth were he soon took his seat next to Selva Pin Pop.

"Now audience please be seated, I know this is a very special night, we are truly privileged to be in your presence tonight Mr. Hendo Wallens. We are about to meet our first contestant, let the show begin," shouted Hip Lee as he waved his hands in the air.

The first contestant entered the stage, it was a boy dressed in a silver jumpsuit. He was going to dance for a hip-hop track, and so he started his dance piece. The crowd was very entertained, the judges seemed to be pleased.... as they moved to the music.

Floza felt very nervous, she started to doubt herself since the first contestant was very good. So, the contestants came on stage one by one, until it was the spoilt girl's turn, she entered the stage happily and she bowed before her performance.

She started playing her instrument, the flute, which sounded beautiful.

"That's the daughter of a wealthy business man," whispered the boy in a magician's costume.

"I am certain that her father has the money to buy off the whole of Durbey, she will surely win."

"I am sure he does," signed Floza. It was a long and a nerve wrecking wait till Floza's performance. Contestant number nine had concluded with his fire eating act. It was now time for Floza to grace the stage.

"Contestant number ten," yelled the show coordinator.

That's me," thought Floza.

"Here it goes, this is for you Father and not forgetting my sweet Rods."

"Welcoming contestant number ten, she goes by the name, 'The Durbey Dancer'."

Floza now entered the stage, the crowd applauded. Before she started, she had noticed Mr. Hendo sitting right before her. He had no clue that it was in fact her, the mask she was wearing clearly hid her face.

The music had started and so she started moving, her dance item started with slow ballet music, and the crowd did not react very well to this. But suddenly the music fused into an electro beat, she started doing her funky moves, in collaboration with her ballet gestures, and the crowd went wild.

"Look its Floza," said one of the lady cats in the hostel,

189

"Look how colorful she looks on stage and her dance is so entertaining."

The judges were impressed by her performance, you could tell because they were all speaking to each other, even Mr. Hendo enjoyed the performance. Little did he know it was the plain old-fashioned girl from Clobet Valley. The voters started calling in, for her performance, up until she had finished her dance item.

Floza finished off her performance with a handstand and a ballet pose. The crowd was extremely pleased with her modern dance performance. Hip Lee walked on stage applauding here. There was so much cheer and excitement from the crowd. Even the judges reacted, they stood up from their seats to applaud Floza.

"And that, Citizens of Durbey, was the 'Durbey Dancer'."

"Should you want to vote for the 'Durbey Dancer' you may call in to one double zero six and vote for performance number ten! Now let us continue with our next performance, the Master of Magic."

"Let's welcome on stage the Master of Magic," shouted Hip Lee.

So, the rest of the contestants completed their performances. There were twenty performances in total, with performers from all parts of Durbey. Hiplee then introduced Rock Cukoo on stage, he was to do a special performance and the crowd really enjoyed it.

"Thank you Rock Cukoo for that amazing performance, and now ladies and gentlemen we have come to the part of the show where we will announce the winner of this year's Durbey Talent show.

But first let us introduce you to the grand prize, the winner of this year's Talent Show will be a lucky winner of the magnificent teleporting bubble. Sponsored by Mr. Hendo himself, the teleporting bubble is one of the greatest inventions of Hendo Enterprises, the lucky winner will have a chance to travel to any part of the world with the use of this handy device. Ladies bring out the grand prize," said the presenter.

Two ladies from backstage brought on stage the teleporting bubble; it was showcased on a glamorous stand.

"Thank you, ladies, and now the moment we have all being waiting for. Let's welcome all our contestants on stage," he said, and all the contestants walked in.

They all drooled over the grand prize; luckily it was placed in a glass casing not to be touched.

"The most votes received from our judges and the citizens from Durbey."

The crowd went extremely silent, awaiting the results.

"The best performance at tonight's Durbey Talent Show, winning by five hundred thousand votes."

"The grand prize winner of the teleporting bubble is the…. The Durbey Dancer!!!!!!"

"Oh, my goodness I have won," shouted Floza. "I am going back home, finally after all the troubles I faced. I am going to see father again, I cannot wait!"

"Can we have Mr. Hendo come on to the stage, to present his sponsored prize to the Durbey Dancer."

"Indeed," said Mr. Hendo, and so he walked to the stage rather studiously, he then took out the teleporting bubble from the case, and walked over to Floza.

"Congratulations, young lady, you are very lucky, very lucky indeed, and he smiled."

"Thank you, Mr. Hendo, I will enjoy using the teleporting bubble," replied Floza.

"Yes, I am sure you will use the teleporting bubble wisely."

"I will!" said Floza as she reached out her hand to receive her prize.

"Ah! Ah, not yet, I think that since you're such a lucky girl, we would like to see your face." said Mr. Hendo.

"Don't you agree audience, would you like to see the Durbey Dancers face?"

"Yes, we would, take the mask off!" shouted the people from the audience.

"What do I do now?" thought Floza.

"I did not expect this, maybe I can make some kind off an excuse."

"Unfortunately, I have come down with a slight rash," said Floza to convince the crowd.

"Rash... oh don't be silly, I would like to see the face of my winner," insisted Mr. Hendo curiously awaiting a reaction from Floza.

Stacy was so excited for Floza, she and the other cat ladies were cheering her on, but silence filled the room, when Mr. Hendo suddenly requested she take off her mask.

"Floza don't do it, don't take off your mask, if Mr. Hendo sees who you really are, he might take the teleporting bubble away from you," panicked Stacy.

Floza stood beside Mr. Hendo, the whole of Durbey awaited her reaction, and she did not have much of a choice. She decided that she would follow Mr. Hendo and the people of Durbey's request.

So she took off her mask, and all were so thrilled to see the face of the Durbey Dancer. All but Mr. Hendo. He was stunned on seeing the face of Floza; he reached for the teleporting bubble and awarded it to Floza. He did not have much of a choice after all the whole of Durbey was watching this scene.

As he gave the prize to her, he stared cunningly at her; it was a look of revenge, and at that very moment Floza felt that Mr. Hendo would not spare her. He walked away from her, in a fit of rage, he ordered his guards to escort him back to Hendo Enterprises, and he flew off in the helicopter he had arrived in. Whilst Mr. Hendo travelled back to Hendo enterprises, he thought of the deceit Floza had brought to him. He had no idea that she aimed to win the teleporting bubble. Now it was his very own invention that would ruin his plan, to get revenge on his enemies.

"This is madness, she tricked me, that foolish girl," shouted Mr. Hendo. "I can't let her get away with this, she has the bubble, she could leave for Clobet Valley at any time. We must turn back, take me to the women's hostel at once!"

"Yes Mr. Hendo, replied the Conploy," driving the helicopter.

CHAPTER 15

THE BRAVE ESCAPE

Meanwhile in Clobet Valley it was the night of the annual fair, the elders were busy planning their exit from Clobet Valley. However before their trip to Durbey, they would cast the spell of protection over the valley. So, the elders went to the old cave, were Master Gillian's magic book was hidden.

"Look at the cave, it shines so bright," said Mr. Thimble as he walked towards the cave.

"Yes, it is ready for its Master, but we cannot leave until we master the spell of protection over the Valley," replied Loops.

"We need to chant the incantations all together, all have to be focused when casting the spell."

So the elders made it to the old cave. It was very cold and dark, so they carried lanterns to light their way. The magic book was hidden behind one of the rocks. It was clearly seen as it glowed beams of light beneath the rocks.

"There it is," said Mrs. Poppsy, underneath the rock. So Thimble and Loops picked up the rock and carried the book. They placed it on a surface, it was quite heavy. Dr. Hoppins opened the book, to find the spell of protection.

"Here it is, the spell of protection, but remember friends, once we cast the spell, we have to leave Durbey immediately."

"But how will we get to Durbey?" asked Headmaster Nimble.

"There is a spell of time travel, this will transport us to Durbey but we have to be specific."

"Where shall we land in Durbey?" asked Dr. Hoppins. "How about the old museum?" asked Loops.

"That might be the best place to land, and so we will use the old museum as our destination."

"Mrs. Poppsy you may assist to cast the spell of protection, but you need to leave the circle when I tell you too."

"Yes Doctor, I will stay behind and see to the people of Clobet," replied Mrs. Poppsy.

"It's time," said Dr. Hoppins, we need to stand around the book.

The elders stood around Master Gillian's magic book, there was immense power felt from the book. It was many years since the friends, had used the book, and since this was a matter of life and death, the book had to be taken back to Mr. Hendo.

"Chant after me, friends," shouted Dr. Hoppins.

We cast your protection over the valley, none shall pass the shield of protection. If he does so, we shall be summoned, the masters of the spell. Light of protection shield Clobet Valley, none shall enter, none shall leave.

As the elders chanted, a light of protection was cast over the sky, over the entire valley. It looked like a shield of color, since the Clobet fair was taking place many of the people had seen the reaction in the sky, but they had thought it was a display as the elders had communicated.

"Now, Mrs. Poppsy leave the circle," shouted Dr. Hoppins.

"Yes Hoppins, please be safe and bring back my Popsicle," yelled Mrs. Poppsy.

We are the circle of light; may the book take us to Durbey.

On chanting of this incantation, the elders started fading.

Take this circle to the museum, to Durbey we must go.

It was in completion of the incantations that the elders disappeared completely, Mrs. Poppsy was left alone; she felt very worried for her friends and she hoped for the best, that Floza and her dear Popsicle would return safely.

Meanwhile at the women's' hostel, all the lady cats were cheering the return of Floza with the teleporting bubble. They were so excited, the lady cats decided to carry her through the hostel.

"Floza you did it, I knew you could!" yelled Stacy. "You can now go home. Can you take me with you?

I will promise to be good."7

"Oh Stacy, of course, we will go back home together, father will be so glad. I will tell him all about how you have helped me. I could not have done it without you!"

"Come let us go to a quiet place, we can try the bubble, maybe we can visit Galley town, the place you grew up in," said Floza.

"No, Floza. We can visit Galley Town some other time.

You must be tired, we should go to bed," said Stacy.

"We will leave for Durbey first thing tomorrow morning, said Floza. We cannot wait much longer, Mr. Hendo knows that I have won the teleporting bubble, he will be here for me tomorrow. But when he comes to the hostel, we will be gone to Clobet Valley."

"Yes, we will be gone from this horrid place," replied Stacy.

"I cannot wait to see Clobet Valley, I hope the people don't get too scared of me."

"I am sure they will love you, maybe you could live with Mrs. Poppsy. She could use a friend."

"Mrs. Poppsy needs a friend does she?" said a loud voice.

Stacy and Floza turned around; to their surprise it was Edor. He had come to the hostel to confront Floza about the bubble and take it away from her.

"Did you think I would let you get away with my teleporting bubble, girl?" he said.

"Edor!" yelled Floza, "What are you doing here?"

"I have come for my teleporting bubble, hand it over or your friend Stacy will be no more," said Edor.

The Conploys got hold of Stacy. What would Floza do now? She was out numbered, how was she to escape Edor and his Conploys?

"I am surprised to see you Edor, or shall I say Mr. Hendo Wallens," she said.

"It seems you fear my human form, much more... so Edor changed into his human form. My name is Mr. Hendo Edor Wallens, pleased to meet you."

He held out his hand to shake hands with Floza. Floza was amazed by how different Edor's human appearance was;

he seemed so dark as a panther. He looked so much more cheerful in his green colored suit and bow tie.

"So this is the real you?" asked Floza. "I am amazed to see a human standing in front of me. Why did you hide your true form?"

"Who's to say this form is true?" asked Mr. Hendo. "Edor Wallens Hendo the most famous and powerful man in Durbey. This is who I really am, as a panther or as a man irrespective of my form, I am the most powerful. So girl? Are you satisfied? Now hand me the teleporting bubble or I will take it from you forcefully."

"No wait, I have a preposition for you," said Floza. She panicked with the sight of the Conploys and Mr. Hendo Wallens, insisting for his teleporting bubble back. She had to act fast, but what could she do?

"Is there a way for me to control the device, vocally?" she thought. "I will have to try."

"Please release Stacy you are hurting her," cried Floza.

"Loosen her, but don't lose sight of her," ordered Mr. Hendo.

"Yes Mr. Hendo," replied the Conploys, releasing Stacy from their grip.

"I have now listened to you Floza, now you listen to me!" yelled Mr. Hendo.

"I have to try this, or I will never go back home," thought Floza. She looked at Stacy as to give her a sign. It seemed like they were both thinking the same thing, at least they were ready to react.

Floza pressed a button to activate the devise, and without Mr. Hendo noticing, she then nodded at Stacy. Stacy ran to Floza immediately. She then yelled on the top of her voice, "Take us to Clobet Valley," and the bubble expanded immediately with Floza and Stacy inside it. The bubble then disappeared into thin air. Mr. Hendo could not react in time,

Floza had vanished within seconds, and she was on her way back to Clobet Valley.

To Be Continued...

Index

Finito di stampare nel mese di marzo 2020
presso Rotomail Italia S.p.A. - Vignate (MI)